David crawled toward Maya, praying that she wasn't dead.

He cradled her head in his arms and held her, checking for a pulse. She was still alive.

Her eyes fluttered open.

"David." Her voice was weak and her gaze unfocused.

"Yes, I came for you." He looked all around. "Did you fall?"

"The man with the knife...he came after me."

"Where is Sarge?"

He'd have to deal with finding Sarge second. First he needed to get Maya to a safe place. "I got you now, Maya. You're going to be okay."

ALASKA K-9 UNIT

These state troopers fight for justice with the help of their brave canine partners.

Alaskan Rescue by Terri Reed
Wilderness Defender by Maggie K. Black
Undercover Mission by Sharon Dunn
Tracking Stolen Secrets by Laura Scott
Deadly Cargo by Jodie Bailey
Arctic Witness by Heather Woodhaven
Yukon Justice by Dana Mentink
Blizzard Showdown by Shirlee McCoy
Christmas K-9 Protectors by Lenora Worth and Maggie K. Black

Ever since she found the Nancy Drew books with the pink covers in her country school library, **Sharon Dunn** has loved mystery and suspense. Most of her books take place in Montana, where she lives with three nearly grown children and a hyper border collie. She lost her beloved husband of twenty-seven years to cancer in 2014. When she isn't writing, she loves to hike surrounded by God's beauty.

Books by Sharon Dunn

Love Inspired Suspense

Broken Trust
Zero Visibility
Montana Standoff
Top Secret Identity
Wilderness Target
Cold Case Justice
Mistaken Target
Fatal Vendetta
Big Sky Showdown
Hidden Away
In Too Deep
Wilderness Secrets
Mountain Captive
Undercover Threat
Alaskan Christmas Target

Alaska K-9 Unit

Undercover Mission

Visit the Author Profile page at Harlequin.com for more titles.

UNDERCOVER MISSION

SHARON DUNN

LOVE INSPIRED SUSPENSE
INSPIRATIONAL ROMANCE

Special thanks and acknowledgment are given to Sharon Dunn for her contribution to the Alaska K-9 Unit miniseries.

LOVE INSPIRED® SUSPENSE
INSPIRATIONAL ROMANCE

Recycling programs
for this product may
not exist in your area.

ISBN-13: 978-1-335-72245-4

Undercover Mission

Copyright © 2021 by Harlequin Books S.A.

This edition published by arrangement with Harlequin Books S.A.

For questions and comments about the quality of this book, please contact us at CustomerService@Harlequin.com.

Love Inspired
22 Adelaide St. West, 40th Floor
Toronto, Ontario M5H 4E3, Canada
www.Harlequin.com

Printed in U.S.A.

There is no fear in love; but perfect love
casteth out fear: because fear hath torment.
He that feareth is not made perfect in love.
—*1 John* 4:18

For Ariel, my beautiful, creative, funny daughter.

ONE

K-9 officer Maya Rodriguez took in a sharp breath as she stepped out onto the quiet upper deck of the Alaska Dream cruise ship. A fog had rolled in making it hard to see more than a few feet in front of her. Maya's partner, Sarge, a Malinois was by her side. He looked cute in his service dog vest. All part of the disguise for their undercover work. Though he was two years old, he was small for his age and breed, and people often thought he was still a puppy. Size was deceptive, however. Sarge was a top-notch detection and screening K-9. His nose could sniff out almost anything—weapons, explosives, even infectious diseases.

Maya's footsteps seemed to echo as she surveyed the boardwalk. Two nights ago, a woman had been murdered on this deck—an entertainment employee for the cruise line. There had been another attack on the ship as well. That victim, a female passenger, had been grabbed from behind. Her attacker held a knife to her throat, but she had managed to get away with only minor injuries. Both victims had similar profiles: young, dark haired, slender and attractive. Maya also fit that description, which was why her boss, Colonel Lorenza Gallo, had picked her for this covert assignment. Though she had been on the K-9 team for five years, this was the first time she'd been undercover.

The cruise ship owner was worried about losing business due to the attacks, so everything had to be on the down low. Ship security had not turned up any suspects or substantial evidence, which in itself was concerning. There was some speculation that the security team was covering for someone or just couldn't do a good job when it came to serious crime on board a ship.

It was so quiet Maya could hear Sarge's paw steps as he heeled at her side. Fear fluttered through her when her hand touched the hip where her firearm would normally be. No guns of any kind were allowed on board, which meant that if she was truly in danger, her only protection was her training and Sarge.

Though they were on the highest viewing area on the ship, she could hear the waves lapping against the hull of the ship. Despite it being June, the Alaska night air chilled her skin.

The clatter of footsteps caused her to whirl around. Her heart pounded. Sarge took up a position beside her, standing at attention and letting out a little supportive yipping noise.

A man and a woman in fancy dress emerged from the fog laughing.

Their expressions grew serious when they saw Maya and her dog.

"I was sure we would be the only ones up here in this kind of weather," the woman said as she circled her arm through the man's elbow.

"Just thought I'd get a little air and solitude," Maya explained. She had seen on the ship's list of activities that there was ballroom dancing this evening. No doubt, the couple had just come from there.

Both the man and the woman drew their attention to Sarge.

The man tugged at the bow tie he wore with his tuxedo. "There's plenty of room on the ship. It's way colder up here than I thought it would be. Enjoy having the deck to yourself, miss."

"Ta-ta," the woman said. Their laughing and joyous mood resumed as they disappeared into the fog. Maya heard a door open and shut.

"False alarm," she murmured to Sarge. "They looked happy, like they were in love." She shook her head. "Some of us are just terminally single, right?" Maya continued to walk the deck looking for the place where the crime report said the murder had taken place. Though all the evidence of the crime had been removed, it often helped to retrace the steps of the victim. She had very little to work with based off the report written by the ship's security chief.

Crystal Lynwood, the murder victim, had worked for the onboard entertainment venues for less than a year. Her body had been found by the east entrance door. She'd been stabbed.

Maya located the door and reached for the knob, preparing to retrace the steps that the victim must have taken.

A hand grabbed her from behind and pulled her back. Judging from the strength he exhibited, the attacker was male. Sarge barked. The man kicked a deck chair in the direction of the dog. Maya heard a yelp of pain.

She felt herself being dragged. She crashed into another deck chair and then her assailant circled around and pushed her from the front until her back was against a wall. Before she could react, he slammed a fist in her solar plexus causing her to wheeze and gasp for breath.

He put a knife to her throat. With his free hand he pressed hard against her stomach. She was still fighting for air from the blow he'd struck. The attacker wore a ski mask.

She could hear Sarge but she could not see him. Why wasn't he coming to help her? As the K-9 barked, she could hear the noise of one object clanging against another.

"I'm going to make you pay for what you did." The man's voice held the threat of violence.

She could feel the pressure of the knife against her throat. Her hands were free. Though he had her pinned in place, she might still be able to get away. She balled her hand into a fist preparing to land a blow to his stomach. He pressed the knife deeper into her skin. She smelled the coppery scent of blood, and her skin stung from the cut.

"Don't even try," he warned.

Sarge's barking grew louder and then there was an odd scraping sound.

The guy shifted and let up pressure on her neck. In that moment, his face was caught in one of the lights that illuminated the deck. She saw green eyes.

Some distance away, she heard footsteps. The attacker glanced to one side and then the other. He lifted the knife off her throat and then without another word disappeared into the fog.

She could hear his retreating footsteps even as the other set of footsteps came toward her.

She didn't see Sarge anywhere—or hear him. Worry gnawed away at her. What had happened to her partner? She called his name. Now she heard the footsteps again coming toward her from the opposite direction the assailant had run to.

A silhouette of a man in uniform emerged from the fog. He held on to Sarge's leash.

"Did you lose your service dog, ma'am? His leash got tangled up with a deck chair and then that chair caught on another one when he tried to drag it and was trapped." The man stepped closer. "I'm the Security Chief, David Garrison." She'd noticed him when she'd boarded this morning. David Garrison was the one who had written the report that gave her almost nothing to work with.

Her chest hurt where she'd had the wind knocked out of her. The cut to her neck, though not deep, still stung. She held her hand out. Sarge jerked away from the man and ran toward her. She struggled to speak. "I—I was attacked."

David's voice filled with concern as he stepped toward her. "You okay?"

She managed a nod. And then kneeled and wrapped her arms around Sarge. Holding the dog steadied her nerves. They both had had a scare.

Officer Garrison straightened his spine and squared his shoulders. "Which way? Where did he go?"

She pointed in the direction the perp had gone. David took off running. Sarge, who was trained to detect weapons and would pick up the scent of the fleeing man as well as the knife, would be able to track even more precisely than the security officer. She commanded him to go. He put his nose to the ground and then lifted his head and sniffed the air. A moment later, Sarge also took off running while she held on to the leash.

David Garrison's footsteps echoed as he darted all along the deck. It didn't take long for Maya and Sarge to catch up with him.

Her partner alerted on the west door that led down to the next deck. She swung the door open. Sarge scampered down the stairs. This floor was comprised of state rooms for the guests. The rooms had balconies that faced inward providing a view of the main floor where there was a pool and bumper cars as well as many shops. She had studied the layout of the ship from the maps provided on each floor, but it was massive. Ten floors of shops, restaurants, entertainment venues and staterooms. It was hard to remember where everything was.

Getting ahead of David, Sarge stayed on the scent, hesitating only a moment as they worked their way down the floors. He ran through the botanical gardens and then came to the door that led to the second deck which was mostly utilitarian and storage. Laundry and cooking facilities, as well as where the medical, administrative and security offices were held. When she peered over her shoulder, she saw that the security officer was behind them. He ran toward her favoring one of his legs with just the hint of a limp.

Sarge came to stand outside a set of double doors that were labeled Main Kitchen.

Maya commanded her partner to stop. The dog sat beside her feet. She turned toward David as he approached. "I think your man ran into this kitchen."

"Oh really. Your service dog knows how to track, does he?" Suspicion colored his words.

"He's protective of me is all." But even to her own ears, her excuse for Sarge's obvious expertise sounded lame.

David was at least six inches taller than her. Brown hair stuck out from beneath his cap. She had to admit he was good looking. Could she trust him to let him know she was undercover?

She caught herself. No matter what, she had to be on her guard. At this point, both passengers and crew were suspects. And she couldn't rule out members of the security team, especially because David's report had turned up zilch. Was he somehow involved?

"The kitchen is shut down at this hour. They start to prep for breakfast in a couple of hours. For sanitation reasons, your dog can't go in." He looked right at her. His eyes were blue. "Despite your dog's apparent talents, we do have regulations."

Okay, so David Garrison was way smarter than his handling of the investigation had let on. He was already suspicious of her story. And the blue eyes and the fact that he had appeared so quickly after her attacker fled probably meant she could take him off the suspect list. But he could still be covering for someone.

"I'll wait outside here with Sarge," she said. "My service dog."

"I can handle this. Why don't you go to the infirmary and get treated for that cut on your neck? I'll get a statement from you later, a description of anything you can tell me about the attacker. I'm sure you're pretty shaken up right now."

She detected the tone of challenge in his

voice. He clearly didn't like a civilian interfering with his law enforcement duties.

"The cut is superficial. I can deal with it myself later. I'd rather just wait here and make my statement right away."

He stared at her long enough to make her feel uncomfortable. She didn't want to blow her cover after being on this boat for less than a day. She'd boarded when the ship had gotten into port in Juneau after leaving Seattle.

"Suit yourself." David pushed open the swinging double doors.

She could see him through the oval-shaped windows as he searched the place.

Maya sighed. She'd been running on adrenaline since the attack. But now that she had a quiet moment to reflect, all the fear she'd suppressed flooded through her. A knife had been held to her throat. She gripped the door frame trying to catch her breath. Sensing her change in mood, Sarge whimpered at her feet and stared up at her. She looked down at his mostly black nose framed by tan around his eyes. The dog was always tuned in to her emotions.

Sarge thumped his tail. His way of reassuring her.

She bent over and stroked his ears. "So glad you're my partner."

Maya straightened up. Her heart beat a little faster as she stared down the long empty hallway, wondering where the attacker had gone. Had he run into the kitchen as Sarge's nose had indicated or was he still lurking close by? As she stood alone in the corridor, she could not shake the feeling that she was being watched.

David Garrison switched on the lights and surveyed the entire kitchen. Stainless steel counters gleamed. The ship had many cafés and eateries, but much of the food was prepped in this main kitchen and then sent up to the other decks. In another couple of hours, it would be bustling with activity as breakfast preparation got underway.

He walked toward the ovens, checking underneath counters. As the ship's head security officer, even he was not allowed to carry a gun, only a Taser. Not being armed to do his job was an adjustment in comparison to the life he'd led as an MP in the army. David clenched his teeth. An IED had ended his grand military ambitions, leaving him with a leg injury.

He thought about the beautiful woman standing outside the door waiting for him. Something about her and that so-called service dog was really off. He wondered if she had noticed that he favored his left leg. He shook his head. Why did it matter anyway?

There were two doors on opposite sides of the kitchen as well as a service elevator for the transport of food. If the attacker had come through here, he could have gotten away. He searched the pantry and opened the service elevator. Finally, he checked the other door down the long hallway.

Well, if the guy had gone through here, he wasn't here anymore. David worked his way back through the kitchen. Now to deal with the woman and her dog…

She was standing in the hallway when he pushed open the door.

"Find anything?"

He shook his head. "What makes you think your dog would know where he went?"

"He was a K-9 before he became a service dog. He knows how to track and detect weapons."

Okay, so maybe that sounded believable. But why not just tell him that in the first place. "What did you say your name was?"

"Maya Rodriguez."

He wondered why she needed a service dog. She didn't have any apparent disability so it might be for emotional support or nonvisual condition.

"Maya, why don't I escort you and your dog back to your room, and you can tell me anything you remember about the attacker," he said. "If you feel comfortable with that."

She nodded. He turned, and they started to walk. It wasn't lost on him that with her long dark brown hair and youthful appearance, Maya looked like the woman who had been murdered and the passenger who had been attacked. Crystal Lynwood, the actress who had been killed, was still wearing an expensive gold-and-diamond bracelet when her body had been found by another crew member. The motive wasn't robbery, which made him worried that they were dealing with someone who was psychologically unstable. It frustrated him that he'd had pressure from the owner of the cruise line to do the investigation quickly.

As they walked, the dog took up a protective position wedging himself in between Maya and him. The canine's black ears stood up as he padded along.

"What did you say your dog's name was?"

"Sarge."

They took a flight of stairs, stepping out onto the promenade, the central part of the ship. The shops were closed at this hour, though some of the entertainment venues and midnight buffets were still open. "What deck are you on?"

"My room is on the sixth floor."

"We can take the elevator." He pointed off in a corner.

"This ship is so big. By the time I learn where everything is, the cruise will be over."

They walked past a music venue where the strains of Broadway tunes spilled out. "True, I think you could keep yourself entertained without ever going ashore."

They got into the glass elevator which faced outward and provided a stunning view of the dark rolling sea as well as the glaciers and mountains in the distance. Though he missed the excitement of the military, the thing he liked the most about his job was how the scenery was always changing. The last thing he wanted was to put down roots anywhere. This ship was his home now. That suited him fine.

Both of them stared out at the landscape. "Can you tell me anything about the attacker? You said he had a knife?"

She let out a heavy breath. "I only saw it for a moment. I would guess that it was more of a hunting knife than something you would use to cook with."

They were still waiting on the forensic autopsy for Crystal Lynwood. All he could conclude from the crime scene was that she had been stabbed. Just like with an airport, all passenger and crew had their luggage run through a screener. How had someone managed to smuggle a hunting knife on board?

The elevator came to a stop, the doors slid open and they stepped out into a carpeted hallway.

"I'm just down that way. Five staterooms away."

Maya seemed pretty calm, so he decided to press her for more information. The best time to do an interview was as close to the crime as possible. Trauma and time tended to distort memory. "What can you tell me about your attacker's appearance?"

"He was wearing a ski mask. Average height and build, nothing distinct about his voice."

Again, David felt a hiccup in his assessment of Maya. The way she was describing the perp was very cop-like.

She stood outside her room. Sarge sat at her feet and looked at David with probing dark eyes. One thing was for sure, the dog was protective of her.

She pulled her card key out of her pocket. "There was one thing about him that was distinct."

"What's that?"

She met his gaze. "He had green eyes. If I saw them again, I would know it was him."

Something about the way she looked at him made him want to lean closer to her. He squared his shoulders remembering that he was on the job. "That's helpful." Though he didn't want to tell her about the previous attack and Crystal's murder, both of which he was sure were committed by the same perp, she had given him significant information. "Why don't you try to get a good night's sleep?"

"Oh, I will," she said.

Again, something in the way she spoke suggested she intended to do the quite the opposite. Why did he keep going back to the idea that she wasn't being forthcoming with him? His dating history had created a natural distrust of women; they always ended up being deceptive in some way. And he understood that that colored every interaction he had with women. Still, he could not shake the gut feeling that Maya was withholding something from him.

She swiped her card key and offered him a smile. "You have a good rest of your night too."

She and her dog stepped inside. The door eased shut behind them. But he didn't hear the dead bolt click into place. Odd. After an attack like she had endured, most passengers would have secured every lock available.

David headed down the hall, turned a corner and continued to walk. He slowed and then stopped. Something was not sitting right with him. Maya Rodriguez was hiding something from him. He turned back around and headed toward the hallway where her room was. He got there just in time to see Maya and the dog headed up the hallway around a corner.

TWO

Maya hurried around the corner with Sarge in tow. She had one more thing she wanted to do before she could sleep— visit the place where the attack on the other passenger had taken place. And she had had to wait until David Garrison was out of the way. Really, he seemed like a nice enough guy, but if she had to be hush-hush about the investigation so be it.

In the report, the passenger had been able to provide no significant information about her attacker, but maybe seeing where the crime had taken place would give Maya a direction to go.

She was sure they were dealing with the same perp. And that that man had probably also attacked her. As she ran toward the elevator, she remembered what he had said.

I'm going to make you pay.

The words gave her chills. But they didn't make any sense. She'd boarded the ship only this morning. Why would someone already have an ax to grind with her?

She stepped into the elevator. The other attack had taken place on the eighth floor solarium. Before the elevator doors closed, a man raced toward it and stepped on. Her heart beat a little faster. The guy was of average height and build. As they both stared straight ahead, she couldn't see what color his eyes were. All the same, being alone with a stranger in a closed space she couldn't escape from made her aware of the need to remain on guard.

"Which floor?"

"Eight, just like you." He stared straight ahead as the elevator numbers lit up.

Sarge let out a low-level growl and then moved so he was in between her and the man.

"Your dog is well behaved, I assume."

"When he wants to be." Maya hoped her comment would deter the man if he did have sinister intent. She glanced sideways at him, taking note of his indistinct appearance.

The ride up two floors seemed to take forever. Finally, the door slid open. The guy moved back to let her go first. She and Sarge stepped out. While she checked the map on the wall for how to get to the solarium, the man stepped out of the elevator and turned down a hallway. His footsteps faded. So he probably wasn't up to anything.

Maya let out a breath. The attack on the upper deck had made her feel vulnerable.

She found her way to the solarium which featured deck chairs facing floor-to-ceiling glass. They were in the forward part of the ship. The view at night was breathtaking. The fog had lifted, and she could see stars and a crescent moon.

There was only one other passenger. An older woman covered in a throw who had fallen asleep on one of the lounge chairs. Maya padded softly past her. The solarium wound around in a half circle. The report said the female passenger had come up here late at night for some solitude when she'd been attacked.

Though Maya wasn't sure how much stock she should put into the comment, the victim had mentioned that she had the feeling she was being followed at different times of the day prior to the attack. If that was the case, this perp stalked his victims waiting for the chance when they were alone and vulnerable. A *feeling*, however, was not hard evidence.

She walked around the solarium. She could no longer see the old woman. Up ahead was a door, and she reached for the handle. As she was opening it, a force pressed on her from behind propelling her across the threshold. Amid all the chaos, she dropped Sarge's leash. The door automatically closed. Sarge was on the other side, his barking muffled but intense. Pounding footsteps indicated that the man who had pushed her was right behind her. She found herself outside on a deck with a railing. A blast of cold air greeted her. There was a door at the other end of the deck that probably led back inside. The wind caught her hair and she could hear the waves beating the side of the ship. She turned to face the man who had pushed her. He lunged toward her. The ski mask he wore made it impossible to see his face.

She prepared to land a gut punch to her assailant. He anticipated the move, blocking her hand as she raised it, then pushed her against the railing. Cold metal pressed into her back. She kept waiting for him to brandish the knife, but he didn't.

Sarge was still barking on the other side of the door, and it sounded like he was flinging himself against it.

With a furious intensity she dove at the man, lifting her hand to grasp his mask. But he was too quick for her.

Her assailant swung her around and pushed her toward the railing. She felt the cold metal press against her stomach. When she looked down, she could see the turbulent water below.

He lifted her up, so she was on her tiptoes. The man was strong. Did he intend to throw her overboard? Her heart pounded as her hands gripped the cold railing. She tried to push away from it. Wind whipped her hair around across her face. He held her by the waist and neck. She locked her elbows, putting distance between herself and the railing.

He leaned close and hissed in her ear. "What are you up to?"

Desperation clawed through her. If she couldn't get away, she knew he'd throw her overboard.

A hand grabbed the back of her jacket and lifted her up. She saw only the sea rolling down below.

Please God, help me break free before he kills me.

The sound of the dog's barking alerted David to where he needed to go. Once Maya had turned the corner by her room, she could have gone in one of three different directions. He had wasted precious time looking for her. Though he had pursued her to find out why she'd lied to him, Sarge's urgent barking alerted him to the fact that she might be in some kind of danger again.

He entered the solarium where an elderly woman resting on a chaise lounge chair was just waking up. He ran around the half circle created by the solarium layout. At the other end of the solarium, he saw Sarge barking and bouncing against a door.

He raced across the expanse and flung open the door. Fear shot through him when he saw a man in a ski mask pressing Maya's body against the railing while she struggled to get away. Her front faced the railing while her hands gripped it. "Security, let go of her right now. Back off."

Turning, the attacker saw Sarge and David. He lifted Maya from the waist and pushed her over the railing. Before David could get to him, the attacker ran to the opposite end of the boardwalk through a door.

David made a split-second decision to let the attacker go and save Maya. He couldn't do both.

Maya's hands gripped the railing and David sprinted to where she was hanging on for her life.

"Hold on! I've got you." He reached down and grabbed her wrists.

He pulled her up, and she swung her legs over the railing, falling into his arms.

"I thought I was going to die," she gasped. "You saved me…again." She pulled away and looked up at him.

He felt a bit breathless when she gazed at him with such gratitude. "Maybe we can still catch him." Perhaps it was just the energy he'd expended pulling her up that made him light-headed. He turned his attention to the door where the attacker had run.

"We'll go with you." Maya tilted her head toward Sarge who was standing at attention waiting for instruction. "Sarge can help. People who are running in fear emit an odor that dogs can track."

"Let's go." He turned and pushed open the door.

"Good." She reached up and squeezed David's arm just above the elbow. Then picked up Sarge's leash and commanded him. "Go."

The dog took off running, leading down the passageway and out onto the floor where there were closed shops and seating areas. Only a smattering of other people were out at this hour. Most everyone was asleep or at least in their cabins by now. The dog stopped to sniff around a children's play area. Lots of places to hide.

David shone his flashlight all around the area but saw nothing. They kept searching, Sarge led them up another floor but lost the scent outside an elevator.

David stared at the doors of the elevator. "I guess that's it. I think he's vanished."

"But he's still out there!" she cried.

He picked up on the fear in her voice. He turned to face her. "You've been attacked twice."

"I think he followed me." Her hand fluttered to her head where there was a bruise. "How else would he have found me there alone."

"Maybe I can't catch this guy yet." The frustration he felt came out in his tone of voice. "But I can at least make an effort to keep you safe. If he's been following you, he probably knows which cabin you're in. The room next to mine in crew quarters is empty and there's an adjoining door." He didn't want another woman murdered, not on his watch.

"I suppose that would be wise. Sarge of course will stay with me." Her voice had become monotone. She was in shock.

"Of course," he said. "Let's go gather your things. I can arrange for a bellhop to meet us outside your door." He pulled his phone out preparing to make the call. "We can swing by and pick up your new card key first. I have the key to where they are kept for the crew and the authority to issue them."

She rubbed the cross necklace that she wore around her neck as though she were thinking about her options. And then she nodded as her eyes grew moist.

Compassion surged through him. "You've been through a lot tonight."

She squared her shoulders and lifted her chin. She swiped at her eyes.

He placed his hand on her upper arm, hoping the gesture would offer silent support. He remembered that she had touched him in the same way just a moment before. Her touch had sent a spark of warmth through him.

Sarge let out a whimper of support. Maya smiled down at him. "He's my best buddy. What can I say?"

David made the call to the concierge station. The man who picked up agreed to meet him at Maya's room with a cart for transport.

After picking up the new card key, which took about fifteen minutes, they walked through the corridors of the mostly quiet ship save for the few overnight janitors and people lingering after late-night buffets and the final shows of the evening. They came to her room. From the opposite direction, an older man was pushing a luggage cart toward them.

She swiped her card key, pushed the door open and stepped inside.

Though the door blocked his view of her, he heard Maya gasp. The dog barked in a rapid-fire fashion. He feared the worst as he moved to see what had caused such alarm.

THREE

Maya placed a hand on her chest and fell back against a wall as she stared at the total chaos that had become her room. Drawers were open. Clothes thrown around.

"Everything okay?" David entered the room. *"Whoa."*

Maya tried to take in a deep breath to calm herself. She waved her hand in a slicing motion in the air where Sarge could see it, a gesture that told him to stand at attention and be quiet.

"Robbery, maybe?" David stepped deeper into the room.

Was this connected to the attacks? "Have you had any recently?"

"There is always petty theft and pickpockets." He shook his head. "Breaking into a room is on a whole different level though. Do you have any jewelry or anything of value?"

Maya shook her head and stepped over to where the open drawers with the clothes hanging out were. Was somebody looking for something? Or was this meant to scare her? This did not fit the nature of the attack on the passenger or the murder of Crystal Lynwood.

She remembered the attacker had asked her what she was up to the second time he'd come after her.

The old man who had brought the luggage cart stood outside the door. "Looks like a break-in. Do you need help cleaning up?"

"I'll handle it, Lester," David said. "I imagine you have to get back to man the desk anyway."

"Yes indeed," the bellhop said. "If you're sure you don't want my help."

"We'll be all right. Thanks, Lester."

David's voice seemed to come from very far away as she stared at the mess that had been made of her personal things. Her purse was flung across the floor, its contents emptied. She'd hidden the purse in a drawer beneath her clothes. Maya leaned down to pick up her fake license and a credit card. Nothing in the purse would reveal that she was law enforcement. Ensuring that her cover wouldn't be discovered.

"I can dust for prints. We won't be able to do anything with the results until we're in port though," David said. "Maybe what we should do first is gather up your stuff and get you settled in the room next to me. At this point, I'm very concerned about your safety. I'm even more convinced that you shouldn't stay in this room."

Maya had to battle not to give in to the rising fear she felt. She was a trained officer used to dealing with violence and the unexpected. The hard part about being undercover was not having the direct support of the rest of the Alaskan K-9 Unit When she got a private moment, she would check in at headquarters with an update. There was no clear evidence to link the ransacking of the room to the attacks, but her gut told her they were related. "Yes, let's pack and get out of here."

As David helped her get her things in order, her head started to clear. Something about having him close made all of this easier to handle.

She picked up the items that belonged in her purse and put them back. She found the little sterling silver locket her grandmother had given her underneath a chair. Even though the chain for it was broken, she always carried it with her. Her *abuelita* still lived in Puerto Rico, so Maya got to see her only every couple of years. Because family was so important to her, having that distance between them could be hard even with her parents and siblings here in Alaska. Bottom line…if the motive for tossing the room was robbery, the invader would have taken the locket.

The entire contents of her purse had been dumped. Was he trying to figure out who she was? If it was the attacker who had come into her room, she supposed the fact that she had visited the areas where the murder and the other assault had taken place might make him suspicious about her. Maybe that was why he had asked her what she was up to. David probably was wondering the same thing.

"The door wasn't forced. Who would have the ability to break in here, anyway?"

David tossed the remainder of Maya's clothes in the suitcase that lay open on the table. He shrugged. "Lots of people. A staff member who had access to the card key. Someone who is computer savvy or has access to a master card key. Or perhaps even a passenger who stole a card key off a maid's cart. It doesn't happen often, but it does happen."

They packed up the remainder of her stuff and loaded it on the cart. David directed her to the service elevator which she noted required that he swipe a card key over it to get in. He pushed the cart while she held on to Sarge's leash.

They arrived at the lowest deck of the ship,

where the staff and crew lived. David opened the room for her.

He pushed the luggage cart inside, helped her unload it and then left it in the hallway. "I imagine you're pretty tired."

"Exhausted," she said and then flopped down on the bed. Sarge sat at her feet. Because this part of the ship was underwater, there were no windows in the room.

"Make sure, the door is dead bolted after I leave." The security chief turned to go and then looked over his shoulder. "Remember, I'm right next door."

"Thank you, David, for everything." Though her body was fatigued, her mind was still racing.

He left, closing the door behind him. She rose and clicked the dead bolt into place. Before turning out the light, she took note of the side door that must lead to David's cabin. She slipped under the covers still fully clothed. Sarge lay down on the floor beside her. He would not jump on the bed unless he was commanded to.

She drew her feet up to her chest. From the crime report that she'd read, she'd made assumptions about David that had been way off. He was obviously extremely conscientious about his work.

Maya wondered how much longer she could keep from him why she was really on the ship. He knew that she had been to both the areas where the crimes had taken place and yet he hadn't pressed her. Probably because he'd seen how shaken up she was after nearly falling off the ship. He already suspected something was off with her cover story, and if she told him the truth it would be nice to have his help. She'd have to clear it with her boss, Lorenza, first.

Turning over on her side, she shuddered as she pulled the covers up to her neck. If the man who had attacked her twice was also the one who'd gone into her room, it meant she had an even bigger target on her back.

David slept fitfully. Partly because his leg hurt and partly because he was concerned about the attacks on Maya. He'd see to it that her old room was dusted for fingerprints. There were probably so many sets in that room that it would be hard to come up with anything conclusive. And maybe the guy had worn gloves. Frustration rose up in him. Chasing down fingerprints felt like a time-consuming rabbit trail.

Anyone who worked for the cruise line went through a thorough background check. That meant that the culprit was either a passenger or crew member with no previous criminal history. What would set someone off to start attacking attractive young women with long dark hair? And now the break-in made it seem like Maya was being targeted in an even creepier way.

He closed his eyes welcoming the fog of sleep as his mind finally started to shut down. His last thought was of Maya in the next room and how she had looked at him with those deep brown eyes.

He had long ago given up the possibility of marriage and kids. His own family had been so messed up by his father's alcoholism and adultery that he feared he would repeat the cycle. Even though he'd become a Christian after the IED had ended his army career, he didn't trust himself to be a good husband. He best served his God by staying single.

He drifted off to sleep with Maya's safety weighing heavily on his mind.

Maya woke up early so she could check in with her supervisor about everything that had happened. After showering and getting dressed, she grabbed her phone and prepared to video chat with her boss.

Though the connection was not great, Colonel Lorenza Gallo's face came on her phone screen. "Maya, glad to see you checking in."

Because the nature of undercover work was so uncertain, they did not have an agreed upon time for Maya to update her commander, only the promise that she would stay in touch and let her know if there were any new developments.

The screen glitched a bit. Maybe a room in the belly of the ship didn't have the best Wi-Fi connection.

Lorenza sat in her office chair at headquarters in Anchorage. In the background, Maya could see Denali, Lorenza's older husky lying in his bed in the corner of the room. Her boss put her face closer to the screen. "How is everything?"

"Things are *not* dull. I've been attacked two times since I boarded, and someone went through my stuff in my room."

Lorenza's eyes grew wide. "Are you okay?"

"Physically I'm fine. Just a bump on the head. Of course, I'm a little shaken emotionally."

The colonel ran her fingers through her short silver hair. "Sounds like we hit a nerve letting you go undercover. Do you think it's the same guy who killed Crystal and attacked the other woman?"

"Yes, I do. The first time he went after me it

was with a knife just like with the others. The breaking into my room is no doubt linked to the other attacks. I'm concerned that he suspects I'm law enforcement and he was looking for some kind of ID in my room. Whether he figures out I'm a cop or not, my being here has caused him to escalate so maybe we can draw him out before anyone else gets hurt."

Lorenza's expression softened. "Maya, please be careful."

The maternal tone of the older woman's voice touched Maya deeply. "I will. I know how to protect myself. It helps that Sarge is with me." She reached over to rub her dog's ear.

"I want you back on land so you can give us a hand with everything we have going on."

"Thank you. The hardest thing about this assignment is being separated from the rest of the team. I miss working the investigations together. Have there been any breakthroughs in the other cases we're dealing with?"

When Lorenza glanced off to the side, Maya figured she must be looking at her laptop. "Actually, we might have something hopeful with our missing bride case. Someone called the tip line. A woman matching Violet's description was spotted in downtown Anchorage."

"Really." Maya felt her spirits lift. At least there was some progress with that investigation. Two months ago, a wedding party had been visiting Chugach State Park outside of Anchorage with a tour guide. The bride, Violet James, along with her bridesmaid, best man and groom all disappeared. The tour guide, Cal Brooks, was found shot dead. Maya and Sarge had been part of the K-9 search party that had been sent to track down the bridesmaid, and later, after their team rescued the terrified young woman, the groom and best man were located as well. Violet James was still at large.

According to the groom, Lance Wells, Violet had shot the tour guide because they were having an affair and Cal was about to spill the beans to Lance. Maya had found an engraved watch that belonged to Lance close to where the bridesmaid had been pushed off the cliff, which made her wonder if maybe the groom was not the innocent victim he said he was. Still, they needed more evidence.

"We're following up on the tip and seeing if there was any surveillance footage in the area where Violet was spotted," Lorenza said. "So, I'm hopeful we'll catch her soon."

Maya heard Denali let out a quick bark off screen. The noise caused Sarge to come to attention and whimper. His tail wagged when Maya looked in his direction.

She smiled at her partner. "You heard your buddy talking, didn't you?"

"I think some of the other officers must be on the floor. Denali always lets me know." A door opened off screen. Lorenza looked off to the side and said something Maya couldn't hear to whoever had stepped into the office. She turned back to look at Maya. "Hunter and Juneau are here. You want to say hi to them?"

Maya clutched the phone a little tighter. "I'd like that."

"Hey there." Hunter McCord's face came into view. Though she could not see him, Maya imagined that Hunter's Siberian husky, Juneau, was probably doing a sniff patrol of the office before greeting Denali.

"Good to see you." Her heart surged. She hadn't realized how much she missed the rest of the team.

Hunter offered her a warm smile. "How's the undercover work going?" For some reason, the image of David and his electric blue eyes popped into her head.

"Not as fun as working with you and Juneau." Hunter had been one of the other officers to conduct the search for the missing wedding party. He had since become engaged to the bridesmaid, Ariel Potter after saving her from certain death when she was held at gun point by a fellow dog breeder who regarded Ariel as competition that had to be eliminated.

Though the jury was still out, Ariel was convinced that Violet was innocent. She'd even received a letter from Violet saying as much. However, as a police officer, Maya had to go by what the evidence suggested. An innocent person didn't usually evade the police like Violet James was doing.

"Hopefully, you'll be back with the rest of the team soon," said Hunter. "Take care." His face was no longer on screen.

Lorenza reappeared. "Keep us in the loop, Maya. Check in when you can. I've got to get to a briefing."

"Okay, bye." She pressed the disconnect button on her phone, feeling a heaviness in her chest. The prospect of undercover work had seemed exciting to her at first. But she hadn't counted on the loneliness. Though she longed to be settled down and married, she didn't have anyone waiting in the wings. With the kind of hours she kept for work, dating was a challenge. She visited her parents and siblings who all lived in Wasilla as often as she could and poured the rest of her energy into work. The K-9 team was really like family to her. No wonder she missed them so much.

Her attention was drawn to the knock on her door from David's room.

Maya smiled when she opened the door. He liked her smile. She was fully dressed in jeans and a pink blouse. Her long dark hair had been pulled up on her head in a braid.

"Sleep all right?"

She nodded. "Sarge needs to go up to the doggie play area and do his business."

"I'll go with you."

"I'm sure I'll be fine. There's lots of people around."

His gut twisted. Her words, which almost seemed to push him away, reminded him that he knew she wasn't being forthcoming with him. If she wasn't a cop, she was hiding something else. Maybe she had some sort of personal connection to the attacker. "I'm going in the same direction."

She shrugged. "Okay." They hurried up to the dog exercise area.

Maya let Sarge off his leash to sniff around and do his business as well as introduce himself to the two other dogs that were there. As a rule, the ship allowed therapy dogs only on board, so the play areas were small.

She had brought a toy with her that she tossed. Sarge retrieved it and brought it to her so he could tug on it while she pulled. The dog growled playfully.

"He plays like a puppy," David said.

She smiled in response as Sarge whipped his head back and forth trying to get her to release the toy. "Some people think he's a puppy because of his size, but he's two years old."

"Yeah, his head looks almost too big for his body."

She let go of the toy and straightened, placing her hands on her hips. "Are you dissing my dog?" Her tone was playful.

"No, not at all," he teased back. "He's cute… in a big-head sort of way."

He liked how bright her expression was and the way light flashed in her pretty, dark eyes. The moment of levity between them made his heartbeat faster. "Let me take a picture of you two looking so cute together." He clicked on the camera icon on his phone and raised it up.

"That would be great. Send it to me so I can show how Sarge and I are having fun on vacation." She stood beside her dog.

A second after he took the photo, his attention was drawn to a scraping sound above him. He looked up just in time to see a huge pot falling straight toward Maya. He leaped the distance between them, pushing her out of the way as the ceramic pot and the plant it contained fell on the ground and shattered. The other two dog owners had grabbed their pets and scooted to the edge of the play area. The few people that were walking around or headed to breakfast stopped and stared. Their gaze going from Maya up to the next deck where the plant had been.

Sarge bounced up and down barking around Maya who lay on her stomach. David rolled off her. "You all right?"

She nodded as she pushed herself up. "Nothing is broken. I'm just a little stunned."

He jumped to his feet. When he looked up, no one was standing at the railing looking down. If the plant had been pushed by accident, it seemed like the person would have stuck around to apologize and make sure no one was hurt.

David took off running. Maya and Sarge were right behind him. He climbed the stairs two at a time to the deck above them. The plant had been one of three arranged outside an eatery that was meant to look like a French bistro with tables outside. There was a closed sign on the door of café. They were not open for breakfast, only lunch and dinner. This early in the morning no one was around.

The other two plants were pushed back from the railing. That meant that someone had to have lifted the pot and tilted it over the railing. Sarge was already doing his thing with his nose to ground where the third pot must have been.

They trotted down the boardwalk past shops preparing to open and where the lifeboats were secured to the outside of the ship. The area opened up to where passengers were doing laps in the pool. There were at least twenty people milling around or in the pool.

The scent of chlorine was heady as Sarge slowed his pace. He circled the pool coming back to where he'd started. Then he paced back and forth and lifted his nose.

Maya shook her head. "I think he lost the scent."

"I'm impressed with his skill…you know for just being a therapy dog."

Color rose up on her cheeks. "I'm hungry. Where is a good breakfast place?"

"Maya you've been attacked three times and your place broken into. I don't think it's wise for you to just randomly go out in the open on the ship. I know this is your vacation, but please, let me see if I can arrange for another security officer to escort you around."

Her lips formed a tight line. "For the whole time?"

"Look, it's a big ship, but this guy can't hide

forever. I have some things I have to do for my job. Why don't I take you back to your room? I can arrange for breakfast to be brought to your cabin. That gives me time to see what I can set up to ensure your safety."

"If we just had something more to go on besides him having green eyes. It seems like once we are in port in a few days, he'll be able to slip off the ship."

David clenched his jaw. "True." She thought like a cop. Why didn't she just fess up to him? The evasiveness reminded him of past failed relationships. Maybe it was his own messed-up family life, but he'd always seemed to pick women who lied, cheated and withheld information. He hadn't dated since he'd become a Christian and he sure wasn't going to start. If Maya not being forthcoming triggered him that easily, it was only more evidence that he needed to stay unattached. "Let me take you back to your room for now. You okay with that?"

She nodded. They walked beside each other with Sarge pulling ahead as they went back down to the crew quarters.

They stood outside her door. "I'll swing by the crew mess hall to put in a breakfast order for you. They can bring it to your room. Then if you could wait in your room until I come by, that would be great."

Her forehead furrowed in frustration.

"I don't want your whole vacation ruined, Maya, but I don't want you dead either."

She sighed. "I know."

"Give me your number. I'll text you with the name of the person who will bring your food… Don't open the door until he or she says who they are."

After she recited her phone number, he waited until she was safe inside her room and he heard the dead bolt slide into place. After stopping by the crew mess and putting in the order for Maya, he hurried up the stairs to the security office. His morning duties had piled up while he'd stayed close to Maya, but it had been worth it to save her life.

David entered the security office. He made arrangements for another security officer to dust Maya's old room for prints and then he opened up the report that the night security officer had filed. It was the usual incidents. Someone who had too much to drink had become unruly, lost jewelry had been reported and missing toys that had been located.

One incident on the report caught his attention. *Woman, Brenda Littleton, age 25 reported that she thought she was being followed as she headed toward upper deck. Officer checked out her claim but found nothing.*

Feeling a lump form in his throat, David called the reporting officer. He knew he would be waking him up, but his gut told him not to wait. The phone rang three times before the other officer, Hans Smith, picked up. "Hello, David. What can I do for you?" Hans's German accent was heavier when he was barely awake. One of the neat things about working on a ship was the international flavor of the crew he worked with.

"Sorry for waking you. I'm just looking over the report you filed for last night. Can you tell me what Brenda Littleton looks like?"

"Is that important?"

David swiveled in his chair. "It might be?"

"Long dark brown hair, pretty, slender," Hans said. "She's not married in case you're interested."

"No, that's not why I asked." A chill ran down David's spine. "Thanks. Try to get some sleep, huh."

He turned off his phone. He stared at the security monitors. Traffic was increasing as guests woke up and looked for things to do. A killer was still out there. Not only was he targeting Maya, but he had to assume that every young woman with long dark hair was still in danger.

FOUR

Maya was getting ready to call her boss to get permission to tell David who she really was when there was a knock on the door. Breakfast had gotten there faster than expected. David had texted her that the server bringing the food would be named Justin.

Maya turned back the dead bolt but kept the door shut. "Who is it?"

"Justin from the crew cafeteria. David Garrison put in a breakfast order for you."

She opened the door. Justin was young, maybe not more than twenty. Her heart beat a little faster when she noted that he had green eyes. Breakfast was laid out on a cart and covered with a silver dome.

"I can take it from here." She had to be careful. The last thing she wanted was to be alone in a room with a man who could be her attacker.

Justin shrugged. She stepped across the

threshold and pulled the cart in. The young man stood staring at her just outside the door. The cart functioned as a barrier between them. She was already making plans to push it toward him if he tried to enter the room. Sarge had moved from his resting place on the other side of the bed to where he was visible to Justin.

"Cute dog." The tone of the server's voice indicated that he found Sarge to be the *opposite* of cute.

Sarge did not wag his tail.

"I like having him around," she said. "For protection."

Justin glanced at the dog and then at her. "You all right?" His forehead wrinkled in confusion.

Maybe he'd picked up on her fear. Maya didn't care if she was coming across as unstable—she wasn't taking any chances.

"I'm fine. Guess I'm a little bit hungry." She pulled the cart in farther out of the way of the door and prepared to close it. "Thank you."

Justin was still watching her as she shut the door and slid the dead bolt back into place. She lifted the silver dome. It looked like David had put in a full breakfast order for her: eggs, bacon, blueberry muffin and orange juice.

After portioning out Sarge's dog food for

him, she settled in and ate most of her breakfast. Then she grabbed her phone and prepared to get in touch with Lorenza Gallo again.

Lorenza's face came on her phone screen but just like before the connection was not great. "Maya, good to see you again so soon. What's going on?"

"Listen, I've got a dilemma. The security chief for the ship has been sticking close to me because he wants to make sure I'm safe, which will make hiding my cover from him hard. And I'm pretty sure he knows I'm not just another passenger." She released a breath. "I know his internal investigation didn't turn up anything, but it's not because he's a clown. David Garrison is actually quite competent."

"Didn't we decide to keep him out of the loop due to the fact that he may have not been thorough in his investigation because he was covering for himself or some other crew member?"

"David has saved my life several times. The one thing I know about our perp is that he has green eyes. David has blue eyes. All of that is to say, I think he can be trusted and I could use his help. Plus, if he can't protect me he'll get another security officer to do it, which will make investigating and keeping my cover almost impossible. I might as well have David's assistance."

Her commander did not answer right away. She stretched and twisted a rubber band she had in her hand, probably mulling over her options. "I trust your judgment, Maya."

"Thank you."

"You caught me as I was on the way out the door. I've got another meeting to get to."

There hadn't been time to tell Lorenza about the potted plant that had almost landed on her. "Okay, bye." Maya pressed the disconnect button on her phone, relieved that her boss had granted her request. At least now she didn't have to be evasive with David. And keeping him in the loop would help with the feelings of isolation she'd been having since she'd taken on this undercover assignment.

A gentle knock on the door jarred her out of her thoughts. "Who is it?"

"It's David."

She walked over to the door and opened it. Maybe it was just her realization of how disconnected she felt from the people she cared about most, but there was something reassuring about seeing the handsome security chief in his crisp white uniform, his blue eyes filled with warmth.

Could she trust him with why she was really on the ship?

"How was your breakfast?"

"It was very good, thank you." Still, she was debating. A wall of tension seemed to go up between them.

"Look, I've got a full day ahead dealing with passengers' concerns. My junior security officer, Noah Lake, comes on duty soon. He has agreed to be your protection so you and Sarge can get out and enjoy the ship."

She could feel a tightening near her heart. She found herself thinking *but I'd rather be with you.* The notion surprised her as she thought David was a bit walled off emotionally even if he did seem to have a high level of integrity and competence where his job was concerned. She stared into his eyes for a long moment and then stepped back. "David, could you come inside? I have something to tell you."

David stepped into Maya's room. He hoped that she was going to tell him who she really was. He didn't like games or secrets. He saw himself as a straight shooter and expected the same of others.

"Please, have a seat." Maya gestured toward a chair and then sat on the end of the bed. Sarge took up a position at her feet. He cocked his head to one side and watched David as he sat down in a chair.

"What is it?"

She let out a breath and straightened her back. "I'm sure you're wondering why Sarge has skills that seem to go beyond that of an ordinary service dog."

"I wasn't wondering too much. I know you said he used to be a K-9, but I'm not buying it."

"Guess I didn't hide it very well," she said. "I am with the K-9 Unit out of Anchorage. As state troopers, we have jurisdiction over all of Alaska. The murder that happened on board took place close enough to the shore that we can investigate."

"So you're here to probe into the murder of Crystal Lynwood?"

"Yes, and the previous attack on the passenger, because the owner of the ship contacted us. Of course, he wants the perpetrator caught and put in jail, but he is also concerned that if the attacks continue his ship will get a reputation for being unsafe."

"My investigation was thorough." A note of defensiveness snuck into his tone. "The owner communicated to me as well the need to keep everything as low-key as possible." He shook his head. "Maybe the need to work quickly without drawing attention hindered my ability to give the case the depth of attention it needed."

"I know that you did the best you could with the restraints you had to work under." She stepped closer toward him. "And I can see that you want to catch this killer as badly as I do."

Her vote of confidence in him lifted his spirits. "Thanks."

She turned to grab her jacket that was laid out on the bed. "I'm sure your junior security officer would do fine watching over me, but I would prefer to hang close to you so we can work this case together. I understand you have regular duties you need to attend to, David, but maybe we can try to piece together who might be behind these attacks in your down time."

He nodded.

"I've seen the reports you filed related to the attack and the murder. But I need to examine them again. What we're looking for here are patterns. Maybe these attacks have been going on for a while, and they are just now escalating for whatever reason."

"I can give you access to those reports and maybe if I look at them it might jar my memory," David said.

"We also need to look at the staff and crew...

maybe narrow it down to who has been here for both attacks."

"There were only minor crew replacements from the time we left Seattle. It could be a passenger too."

"Right now, there is a lot to consider." She blew out a breath. "We need to find a way to narrow it down to a male of average build with green eyes."

"That's not much to go on. Let's get started. You can shadow me in my rounds to answer some of the calls and complaints and we can talk."

Maya tapped a finger against her chin. "People are going to wonder why I'm following you. Let's just say that I am a reporter doing a story about security on a cruise ship." She slipped into her jacket then moved toward the table where Sarge's leash was. The dog was already in his service dog vest.

"All right that sounds like a good cover."

She clicked Sarge into his leash. "I'm going with the theory that my room was ransacked because the attacker was trying to figure out if I was a cop and was looking for some sort of ID. Maybe if he thinks I'm a reporter, he won't see me as such a threat."

"Maybe." David crossed his arms over his chest. "But in terms of appearance, you fit the profile of the other two women. I'm sure that's why you were chosen for the job." It impressed him that she had the level of courage to take on such an assignment, putting herself in harm's way to catch a killer. "One thing we have to keep in mind. If he's not coming after you, he might go after other women. Last night, we had a report of a women who thought someone was following her as she made her way to the upper deck."

"That does seem to be one of his favorite places. I wonder why? Crystal was killed there. And that is where I was first attacked when I went up there to check out the crime scene."

"I don't know…maybe the killer has some personal connection to that part of the ship. It's one of the places that is mostly unused at night," he said. "Too windy and cold even in June."

"Okay. What do we do first? Do you have business to attend to or can we go look at the reports…?" Sarge sat down at her feet and looked up at David.

The two of them were cute together, the big-headed dog and the beautiful dark-haired K-9 officer. "I have a couple of issues to deal with first—a missing purse and a complaint about apparent theft of supplies in one of the eateries."

"Sarge and I are right behind you," Maya said.

They hurried up to the passenger rooms where David interviewed an older woman who said her purse had been stolen while she was ballroom dancing. David took a description of the purse. On their way to deal with the theft at a restaurant, static came across his radio. He pulled it off his belt and pressed the talk button. "Officer Garrison, what is it, Noah?"

"Looks like we got an altercation in the bumper cars. Started out between kids who wanted the same car and escalated to parents, probably alcohol involved. You want me to handle it?"

"I'm close. I'll meet you there. Let's go see if we can settle things down." He turned off his radio and put it back on his belt.

"The fun never ends, huh?"

He liked the way her eyes filled with admiration. "I'm sure it's nothing like the calls you go out on," he said.

"It's all police work, right?"

"Let's go handle this." David took off at a jog. He was aware that the way he favored his injured leg would be more apparent. A wave of self-consciousness swept over him as he made his way through the hallways and corridors of the ship Yet at the same time, he found himself wanting to open up to Maya and tell her all the history that had brought him to living like a nomad on a cruise ship. She seemed like the kind of person who would listen without judgment.

As he rounded the curve, he wondered why he was even entertaining such thoughts.

Maya and Sarge kept pace with David as they came to the open corridor surrounded by shops and then entered the bumper car zone in the sports section of the ship. There was a crowd of people gathered around two men who were facing each other. Though they were not hitting each other, the combative stance—hands curled into fists, chests out—revealed the level of tension between the two men.

Noah Lake, dressed in his security uniform, entered from the other side of the bumper car area.

David turned toward Maya. "Why don't you and Sarge hang back?"

She commanded the dog to sit.

As he approached the two men, the glassiness in both their eyes told him they had been drinking. It seemed a little early to David, but some people thought of the cruise as a nonstop party. Noah closed in from the other side. Though things seemed relatively calm on the surface, he knew from experience that if alcohol was involved, violence could explode at any second.

In an odd way, his childhood served him well in his job. He was always ready for anything.

"Gentlemen, what seems to be the trouble here?"

He noticed then that the shorter man had a bruise on his cheek. Indicating blows might have already been exchanged. The taller man leaned toward the shorter one in a threatening manner. David was like a lion ready to pounce. His heart beat faster as he gave Noah a quick glance.

The taller man never took his eyes off the fellow with the bruised cheek. "This guy tried to take my son's bumper car."

"You liar." The man with the bruised cheek lunged at the other man.

David jumped into the fray and so did Noah as the passengers punched each other. David got between the two men and backed the taller one up while Noah did the same with the other man. "You have a choice here. I won't cuff you if you agree to go peacefully to a detainment area where both of you can cool off and sober up. If you give me any trouble, the cuffs go on."

A woman off to the side with her arm around a boy who looked to be maybe eight or nine spoke to the taller man. "Do what he says, Lee."

The taller man nodded.

"Okay, let's go," David said.

Noah and David escorted the two men away from the bumper cars. They walked past where Maya and Sarge were. Noah looked in Maya's direction. Her face blanched. How odd. Then Noah glanced back at David. It had never registered with David before that Noah had green eyes.

David felt a tightness in his chest. Any of the security officers on the ship would have easy access to card keys that would have allowed them to break into Maya's room. No one was above suspicion at this point.

He didn't like the idea of leaving Maya alone, but he couldn't make Noah escort the two men by himself. There was too much danger of another altercation, and it would break protocol if he did.

As he glanced over his shoulder to see Maya letting a woman and her daughter pet Sarge, he realized he needed to get back to her as quickly as possible.

FIVE

After Maya let the woman and her daughter pet Sarge, she left the bumper car zone, found some outdoor seating and pulled out her phone. The K-9 sat at her feet on full alert. His ears stood straight up as he watched all the passers-by.

If David was taking those two men someplace where they could sleep it off, he wouldn't be able to answer his phone right away. She sent him a text asking if it would be okay if she came to his office and they looked through the police logs together.

Seeing that the other officer, Noah, had green eyes had sent chills through her. The change in David's expression suggested that it had registered with him too.

Maya put her phone away and looked up. She was in an open area of the ship where she could see the sky and the stacked decks with interior balconies where passengers had a view of the activities on the promenade below. She bolted to her feet. Maybe sitting out in the open like this wasn't such a good idea. It would be too easy to drop something from one of the balconies.

She remembered that there was a running track on the third floor of the ship which was one floor above where David's office was. That track was not exposed to the open area. She returned to her room, put on her tennis shoes and texted David about what she was doing. He still hadn't replied to the first text she'd sent, but she knew she needed to be patient. The man did have a job to do.

The run was relatively safe and would get rid of some of her nerves. Sarge as well needed to be exercised. Her place where she lived in Anchorage was close to a park. She often took her partner there to train and expend his energy. The confinement of the ship was hard on a dog who was used to a lot activity and space to move around.

Maya ran up to the third floor and located the track. She took off at a steady jog, seeing no other runners on the track. Sarge kept up with her as she increased her pace until she was gasping for air. The exertion felt good. She'd gone only about half a mile when her phone dinged. She stopped and pulled her phone out.

I'm in my office. Was waiting for Noah to leave.

On my way, she texted back.

After checking the map on the wall, she took off in the direction of David's office, taking several turns through corridors and then going down to the second floor. This part of the ship was like a labyrinth for someone who wasn't familiar with it. She slowed her pace realizing she was lost. She must have taken a wrong turn. Her heart beat a little faster and she knew it wasn't from the running.

There was no one in this part of the ship. She walked past several doors. The signs indicated that they were used for different kinds of storage.

She pulled her phone out and pressed David's number. It rang once.

A body slammed into hers. The masked man. He must have been following her. She caught the glint of a knife right before her back slammed against a door.

Sarge barked. The man turned slightly, threatening the dog with the knife. Sarge kept barking but backed up. The momentary distraction was enough time for her to lunge at the man, reaching for the hand that held the knife.

The man whirled around focusing his energy back on her.

Maya could see Sarge in her peripheral vision as the dog leaped at the masked man and latched onto a pant leg. The dog continued to growl and tug while Maya tried to extract the knife from the man's hand. First by pinching the nerves in his wrist and then clawing at the fist that held the knife. Her nails drew blood, but the man held on.

Laughter and the sound of many voices floated up the corridor from around the corner. The assailant lifted his head to the noise of people coming toward them. He pulled his hand away and pushed Maya against the wall with intense force. Her back slammed against the hard wall and pain shot through her, momentarily paralyzing her.

She watched in horror as the man yanked his pant leg away from Sarge's grasp and then kicked toward the dog's head. Sarge jumped away before the boot could find its target.

The attacker pushed again just as she straightened up. "You and your dog are in my way."

The man took off running as chatter and laughter from the crowd of people came from the other direction. Maya struggled to get a breath while her assailant's words echoed through her head. Now it was clear that he had figured out she was a cop.

At least ten people, some dressed in uniforms for work, came around the corner just as the man who had attacked her disappeared in the other direction. They were so focused on interacting with each other that they barely noticed Maya. As they walked past her through the narrow hallway, blocking the possibility of her chasing the masked man, she doubted she could catch him. Maybe security cameras would show where he had gone. Sarge had moved to sit at her feet where she was still using the wall for support.

The group of people made their way up the corridor and around the corner, their voices growing fainter.

Finally, she was able to take in air and get a deep breath. Her stomach still felt like it was tied up in knots. Sarge offered a supportive whimper. She reached down and patted his head.

Her phone lay on the carpet where she had dropped it close to the opposite wall. She stepped across the corridor to pick it up.

David's voice came from far away. "Maya, Sarge where are you?"

Feeling the sense of relief, she ran toward his voice. She looked around for the sign that would indicate which hallway she was in but didn't see one. "David, we're here."

She heard pounding footsteps and then she saw him as he stepped into the hallway. The tall, handsome man in uniform was a welcome sight. A look of intense concern crossed his features.

He hurried toward her. "What happened? The phone rang—I picked up. I heard pounding noises and Sarge barking."

"It was him. The man in mask attacked me." Her legs felt weak. She fell into his arms and he held her.

"I was afraid of that. I knew you were close to the office, so I went looking. Maya, I was worried about you." His voice wavered from the intensity of his emotions.

His arms enveloped her. She felt safe now.

He pulled away but still stood close to her looking from her toes to her face. "Are you hurt? Do we need to get you medical attention?" His voice filled with concern.

"I'm okay physically. Just very shaken up."

"From now on, you need an escort 24/7. That's all there is to it."

She nodded. If even walking to his office was not safe, he was probably right. Still, she didn't like the loss of freedom and knew it would make conducting the investigation that much harder.

"He must have been following me and waiting for his chance. He'd stick out like a sore thumb with that mask on, so he must have put it on at the last second."

David gazed down at the beautiful dark-eyed woman, trying to take in what she was saying. The fear he'd seen on Maya's face when he'd come around the corner had sent a wave of rage through him toward the attacker.

She glanced up. "There's no security cameras? I thought we might be able to catch him on tape before he put his mask on."

"This floor is mostly for staff and crew. The security cameras are mounted in public areas that the passengers use."

Maya nodded. It was clear from her body language, the tightness in her features, that she was still shaken by the attack.

Why was this murderer constantly able to evade him? Wanting to reassure her, he purged the intense emotion from his voice. "My office is just a couple of twists and turns from here. Let's go sit down, maybe get you a hot cup of tea. We'll talk." He turned and started walking.

"A couple of twists and turns?" Her voice wavered.

He slowed down and offered her an arm for support when she struggled to keep pace with him. Sarge walked a foot in front of them.

"I don't know how you find your way around here," she said. "I keep getting confused especially on these two bottom decks."

"You get used to it," he told her. "The lack of windows on the bottom decks sometimes disorients people. The narrow hallways don't help either, but space is at a premium on the ship."

As she followed David, her mind returned to the case. "If we could figure out why he attacks the kind of women he goes after, that might help us narrow down the possibilities."

"Do you have any theories?"

He turned down another hallway, which brought them outside the security office. David swiped his card key over the locked door and pushed it open, stepping to the side so she could go in first.

She and Sarge walked in. Maya looked at the monitors. "Do you have a view of the entire ship?"

"Cameras are only set up in the public areas. I only have eight monitors—one for each of the decks where the passengers are. I can switch between cameras to show the different areas on each deck." He moved past her and placed his hands on the keyboard to show her how quickly he could click through the different parts of the ship. Then he pulled a chair out for her. Though the color had returned to her face, something about Maya seemed changed from this last attack. The threat was very personal.

He placed a hand on her shoulder. "It's okay to say you're afraid."

She massaged her temples. "I'm a police officer. I should be able to handle this."

"Everyone has a breaking point, Maya. I know I reached mine when I was in the army. How about I get you that hot cup of tea and you can take a moment to collect yourself?"

"Okay." She sat down and nodded, still watching the monitors.

He strode across the room to where there was a two-burner coffee maker. One carafe held coffee that was mostly bitter by this time of day and the other kept water hot. He grabbed a tea bag from the assortment and placed it in a coffee cup.

"You said you were in the military?"

The question made his stomach clench. But he was the one who had brought it up. Though it made him afraid, he wanted to open up to her. Maya had a tenderness that he had never experienced before. He poured the hot water into the cup watching it turn brown.

"I thought I was going to be a career officer." He turned and carried the steaming mug toward her. He placed it on the counter beside the keyboard. Sarge lay at Maya's feet, resting his chin on the toe of her shoe.

She lifted the mug and blew on it but didn't take a sip. "What happened?"

"An IED happened."

"Your leg? I noticed you favor it sometimes." She gazed at him before putting the mug down. "You really can't tell unless you're running."

Her voice held such a tone of compassion and nonjudgment that the tightness in his stomach disappeared. "Thank you for saying that. I worked hard with the physical therapist to get back as much mobility as I could. I guess I have a memory of what I used to be capable of physically."

"Loss is never easy. I'm sure it was hard to reroute your career path."

The way she looked at him made his heart beat faster and that scared him. He jerked to his feet and turned away. "I don't mind it." He shrugged. "I like not being settled anywhere. The scenery and the passengers changing every ten to twenty-one days—it suits me."

"My job has some travel involved but I'm

kind of a homebody." She let out a sigh. "I just had my thirtieth birthday. I thought I'd be married and with kids by now. That was always my dream."

Was she hinting at something? Though his feet remained planted, David felt like he was running a hundred miles an hour and the cavalcade of relationships that had turned sour played out in his mind. "Not me. I like being an unattached nomad."

Her expression changed as she drew her eyebrows together and leaned back. "Oh, I see. We all make different choices...have different dreams."

"Look, why don't we look through those reports? I can tell you off the top of my head nothing comes to mind that resembles these attacks and the murder."

"I just thought if there was something on a previous cruise, we could eliminate the passengers as suspects. You said crew personnel stays the same, right?"

"For the most part. Everyone has a contract, most of which run a year. People go on vacation or get sick, some people quit and we have to replace them," he said. "But I would say the core group of people stays the same."

"We're dealing with such a huge group of

suspects. There has to be a way to narrow our focus," Maya reiterated.

"If we're assuming the attacks only started when we left Seattle. That means both passengers and crew members could be suspects." David shifted in his chair. Green eyes aren't that common, but I still think we're talking about hundreds of suspects."

"The upper deck where I was attacked that first night was a public area. Did the security footage show anything?"

He shook his head. "Nothing. And very little on the night Crystal was killed either."

"Almost like he is aware of where the cameras are."

Feeling a rising frustration, David shook his head. "All passengers and crew members have to have a photo ID, but I don't have software that would sort IDs for green eyes. We'd have to do that by hand. My onboard resources are kind of limited... Sorry."

"That's okay. We'll just have to do good old-fashioned detective work, right?"

He appreciated her optimism since he tended to be a glass half-empty guy.

"Right." David scooted his chair toward a computer. "I can look and see if there were any new hires for this cruise." He clicked the keyboard and looked at the screen. "We had one woman, a waitress named Tiffany Swarthout, who quit right before we sailed. There was not time to find a replacement."

"Okay, so that was a dead end."

Noah's voice rose above the static of the radio. It sounded like he was running. "Purse snatcher fourth floor. Headed toward the third. Let's cut him off."

"On my way," David said. He bolted to his feet.

Maya got up as well, picking up Sarge's leash.

"Where do you think you are going?"

"With you. We agreed I shouldn't be alone, right? Sarge might be a help."

There was no time to argue the finer points of her staying in the locked office. So with Maya and Sarge beside him, David hurried through the corridors of the ship until he came to the elevator that would take them to deck three. They stepped into the elevator.

Maya stood close enough that her shoulder was almost touching his as they watched the numbers light up. Something about her being with him, working beside him, created a sense of peace he hadn't felt in a long time.

Even though he knew that she was a trained

officer who could take care of herself, he felt protective of her. He only hoped he'd made the right choice in letting her come with him.

SIX

Before the number three lit up, Maya stepped toward the closed doors of the elevator. Her heart raced. This was what she loved about police work. The doors slid open, and she, David and Sarge all stepped out in unison.

"There are two or three ways he could go once he gets down here. How will we find him?"

"We block the most likely exit to the second floor. Noah will watch so he can't go back up. He's probably trying to blend in at this point. Which means he may have taken the money out of the purse and ditched it." David got back on his radio while he walked. "Do you have a description of our perp?"

"Yellow shirt. Red shorts. Young and athletic."

A man matching that description would be easy to spot. "Is there a chance he could slip into a cabin? Maybe Sarge and I could search," Maya said.

"No, the deal is you stay close to me." He softened his voice. "I don't want to risk you being attacked again. Plus, searching the cabins is a little more involved legally unless someone is in immediate danger."

His protectiveness touched her.

David came to the stairwell exit that led back down to the second floor.

"He could take the elevator down as well, right?"

"Sure," David replied. "The thing about a ship is he can't go far and his crime was probably caught on the security cameras. It would just be nice to wrap this up and get the purse back to its owner, but we'll catch the guy before we get to the next port."

He got back on the radio. "We're at the north stairwell."

"Far as I can tell he is headed your way based on where I last saw him," Noah said. "He's slowed down and he doesn't know I'm tailing him. I'm hanging back so I don't arouse suspicion."

David signed off and looked at her. "We'll wait inside the stairwell. He'll turn and run if he sees us."

They took up a position on opposite walls

where they could peer out the window on the door that led to the stairwell. Maya studied the area. There was one hallway the perp could veer off into if he realized he was trapped.

A man matching the description of the purse snatcher came around the corner. David stepped out and identified himself. "Security. Put your hands up where I can see them."

Her heart beat faster as she and Sarge stepped out as well.

As she had predicted, the purse snatcher veered off toward the side corridor. She and Sarge chased after him, blocking his escape. Sarge barked only once, but the tone of threat was clear.

"You might want to put your hands up like the security officer suggested," she said.

The purse snatcher complied.

"Hands behind your back." David pulled out the zip ties that sufficed for handcuffs. "What did you do with the purse?"

"I ditched it in the trash."

"And the money?"

"Wallet in my left pocket. Am I going to jail?"

David drew out the wallet. "Theft is still theft even on a cruise ship. You'll wear an ankle bracelet and be confined to your cabin until we reach the next port where you will be taken into custody."

Noah came around the corner and headed up the hallway. "Caught him?"

"Yes," David said. "Thanks to Maya and her dog."

"Why is she hanging so close to you?"

"I'm a journalist doing a story on security on board a ship." It was the first time she'd had to vocalize the deception.

Noah stared at Maya long enough to make her uncomfortable. "You and your service dog make quite a team." His smile didn't quite reach his eyes. "The dog is pretty protective of you... I noticed earlier when I saw you."

What an odd thing to say at a moment like this. Despite the elation and excitement of catching the purse snatcher, she was reminded that a killer was still at large on the ship and she might be looking at him right now.

Her pulse sped up as Noah continued to study her. Maybe he just wasn't buying that she was a journalist or maybe there was something more sinister going on.

She turned toward David. "Do you need to take this guy somewhere?" she asked, purging her voice of the fear that had encroached on her. Right now, no one with green eyes was above suspicion of being a killer.

* * *

David glanced over at Noah after noticing how Maya's expression had changed when he looked at her. Just because he worked with Noah didn't mean they could take him off the suspect list.

"I can take this guy in for processing if you want," Noah offered.

"That would be great." David handed the perp over to the other officer who escorted him down the stairwell.

"I'm too wound up to head back to the security office. We can go grab a bite to eat if you'd like." Maybe it was just the adrenaline from having caught the purse snatcher, but he found himself not wanting to end his time with Maya.

"Are you still on duty?"

"Actually, I was off hours ago," he answered. "Noah still has half a shift to finish and the night guy will be coming on in a couple of hours."

"I could use an early dinner since we haven't had lunch, but maybe we could order in," Maya said. "That way Sarge can eat too."

It would be safer for Maya not to be out in the open. "I like that idea."

They hurried through the corridors of the

ship. David stood outside Maya's door while she slid the card key across the reader.

"Let me have a look around before I leave you here alone to go change out of my uniform."

She stepped aside to let him go in first.

"If there is any kind of new smell in here, Sarge will alert to it." She kneeled and released the Malinois from his leash.

Sarge took off with his nose to the carpet while David checked the tiny bathroom, pulling back the shower curtain, and then he returned to the main room and checked under the bed while Maya opened the closet door. The dog sat back on his hindquarters and looked to Maya for further instructions.

"Just give me a minute to get changed," David murmured. "You can call into the staff kitchen and order something. I'm partial to the chicken parmesan." When she smiled at that last part, he added, "I'll give you the number code for staff to order. There should be a print menu for the staff kitchen in one of your drawers. Ask who the name of your server will be."

"Got it." After David gave her the five-digit number code for ordering, Maya headed across the room.

He had his hand on the doorknob that connected their two rooms. "Maya, remember to dead bolt the door until the delivery guy comes. And ask ahead of time what his or her name is when you order. Get verification that is the person at the door before you open it." He didn't like leaving her even for a moment. Hopefully, he would get changed before dinner even came.

"Will do. Those security measures make total sense." Maya moved across the room and dead bolted it.

David returned to his own room. His time in the military had taught him to live a minimalist lifestyle, which meant his cabin was tidy and uncluttered. He'd noticed that Maya tended to fling her suitcase open and leave clothes and clutter around. As he slipped out of his uniform and changed into something more casual, he wondered why he was even taking note of their different habits and tolerance for clutter. He hung the uniform outside the door so it would be picked up for cleaning and returned.

Then he knocked on the door that separated his and Maya's cabin.

"Come in. Food's on its way."

He opened the door. She had changed into an oversized orange sweater and jeans and she'd unbraided her long dark hair. It was the first time he'd seen her with her hair down.

His heart fluttered at the sight of her. The faint smile she offered him only added to her beauty. Sarge lay at the foot of the bed. Maya had taken his service dog vest off. Though the dog was in a resting pose, his lifted head and straight ears suggested that he intended to be "on the job."

"When the food comes, my cabin is a little bigger and there is a dining area. Maybe we could eat over there."

"Sure, that sounds good."

"These cabins are below the waterline of the ship so I'm sorry we don't have a viewing deck or anything. Not exactly the same experience as the passengers."

"I don't mind. Dinner with you would be nice no matter what."

The comment caused him to flush.

A second later, there was a knock at the door. And a female voice announced, "Room service from the staff kitchen."

"Her name is Angie. You can get the meal if you want to. I'll stay out of the way."

Maya stepped out of view of the door.

David strode toward the door and flipped the dead bolt back. "Thanks, Angie. Much appreciated." He pulled the room service cart inside and then dead bolted the door again. "What did your order?"

"You said the chicken parmesan was good, so I got that too."

Maya held the door open for him while David pushed the cart into his suite. Together they placed everything on the little table and sat down. She called Sarge to come lie at her feet, and after saying grace, they dug into the meal.

David cut his chicken and took a bite, relishing the Italian spices and moistness of the meat. "Our staff chef does this so perfectly every time. Although it does taste a little different. I wonder if he changed the recipe."

Maya took a bite as well. "It's yummy."

They shared small talk about different calls they had been on in their jobs, laughing and enjoying each other's company. Maya was a hearty eater who seemed to enjoy the meal as much as he did.

Midway through their meal, his stomach started to twist. He had the sensation of heat rising up his face. When he looked over at Maya, her face was red too.

"I think something in the food was off."

He ran for the bathroom. He heard Maya's footsteps and she hurried to her own bathroom.

As he flushed the toilet, a dreadful thought entered his mind. They'd been poisoned. Because they both had ordered the same thing, both meals had been tampered with. Still feeling nauseated and weak, he crawled out into the main room and reached for his phone to call the ship doctor.

Through the open door that connected their rooms, he could hear Maya being sick and Sarge pacing and whimpering.

He dialed the number and spoke to the ship's nurse even while his stomach threatened another eruption. "This is security officer Garrison. I'm in my cabin. I think I and a passenger have been poisoned. I need to arrange for transport. There is no way we can make it on our own."

The nurse promised a speedy response.

He clicked off the phone and lay on the floor on his stomach. Sweat broke out on his forehead. He prayed that they were not too late in getting the poison flushed out of their systems.

SEVEN

Feeling weak and nauseated, Maya awoke in a dark room. The last few hours had been a blur. Medical personnel had come for her and David. They'd been transported on stretchers. At some point, she must have lost consciousness or been given something.

Gradually, her eyes adjusted to the dark. There were curtains on either side of her hospital bed, and she was hooked up to an IV. The doctor must have flushed the poison out of her system by pumping her stomach.

A sense of panic made her more alert. What had happened to Sarge? Had David survived the poisoning? She tried to sit up, but the room spun around her, forcing her to slump back down. Her head sank even deeper into the pillow.

She padded the area around her on the bed. There must be a call button somewhere. She couldn't find it, and she didn't have the strength to roll on her side to see if it was on the tray beside her bed.

Footsteps tapped toward her.

"Nurse? Doctor?" Her voice was hoarse and faint. Her throat was raw from throwing up.

The footsteps grew louder coming toward her. A shadow appeared on the other side of the curtain.

"Nurse? I could use some help." She rested her hands on her stomach which wasn't churning anymore but still hurt.

Whoever was outside her curtain didn't respond. Instead he or she walked almost a full circle around her. They got to the place where the two curtains came together creating an opening.

"Hello?"

He or she continued to stand just outside the opening. Maya's heartbeat revved up a notch. She had a feeling whoever was on the other side of the curtain was not medical personnel. Having found out that she'd survived the poisoning, the attacker had come to finish the job.

She summoned all her strength to cry out. "Nurse? Somebody?" Her voice sounded weak. She wondered if anyone would even hear her.

A light came on at the far end of the room. The silhouette of the man outside her curtain retreated. But the footsteps were not rapid, almost as if the attacker were trying to appear casual as he made his escape.

Again, she heard tapping footsteps coming from the opposite direction that the attacker had gone.

A man pulled back her curtain a few inches and poked his head in. "Everything all right here?"

"I..." Talking still took substantial effort. She lifted her hand and pointed in the direction the assailant had gone. "Did you see a man leaving...that way?"

The man shook his head. "I was focused on you. I thought I heard you cry out."

She nodded.

"Is everything okay?" he asked. "I'm the night duty nurse. My name is John."

She nodded. "David Garrison? Is he okay?" She braced for bad news.

"He's three beds over and still unconscious from the sedation. Both of you had a rough go at it. But I think we got you flushed out fast enough."

She relaxed. David had made it.

"We took samples, but we won't know what it was until we can get it to a lab. At first we thought food poisoning, but no one else who ate the chicken parmesan got sick."

Her mind still felt foggy. She'd known right

away that it was poison. That meant between the time the food had been prepared and then brought to her door someone had tampered with it. It was unlikely that a passenger would have had access to the crew kitchen. And how would they have known that she and David had put in an order? That meant that the attacker was a member of staff or crew. As her thinking became clearer, she felt a fresh wave of panic. "My dog?"

John shook his head. "I'm sorry I don't know anything about a dog."

She placed her hand on her chest. "There was a service dog, Sarge." The K-9 was well-trained enough that he would have remained in the room until he was commanded to do otherwise. Her fear was that the attacker had taken the opportunity to harm Sarge since he saw the dog as an obstacle to taking her out of the picture.

The nurse stepped toward her. "I can ask around about the dog. Now why don't you let me take your vitals and then you can get some sleep?"

"I won't be able to sleep until I know that Sarge is okay. How long have I been out of it?"

"It's past nine p.m." John lifted her hand and put a device on her finger to measure her pulse. After he finished checking her blood pressure and her stomach sounds, he turned to go, promising to ask around about her dog.

Maya managed to get herself into a sitting position. She stared at the ceiling and tried to not let her mind wander to all the bad things that could have happened to Sarge. "David? Are you awake?"

"Hey," David's voice sounded weak and far away. All the same, it was a welcome sound. "I just now woke up. Still feel groggy from the sedative."

"Why don't you ask the nurse to open the curtains between us? Maybe they can scoot your bed closer."

"Okay. Just give me a minute. It takes all my brain and muscle power to push the call button and talk."

She let out a breath that sufficed for laughter. "I know the feeling."

While she waited in the near darkness, she prayed for Sarge's safety. The bond to her partner was just as strong as if Sarge had been human. The thought of anything happening to him filled her with despair.

It was hard enough to be away from the rest of the K-9 unit. To not know if Sarge was okay was heartbreaking.

She heard the patter of footsteps and the

sound of David's voice though he spoke in such a low voice she couldn't understand his words.

A few minutes later a different nurse, an older woman, and John were pulling curtains out of the way. Seeing David two beds over lifted her spirits. He offered her a wave and a faint smile.

Together the two nurses worked to get the empty bed out of the way and push David's hospital bed closer to Maya. They turned on the lights over her bed.

"Don't visit too long," John said. "Both of you need your rest. Your bodies have been severely traumatized."

"Any news on Sarge?"

"The dog was not in the room. We're still trying to track down what happened to him."

Her fear came back tenfold. Sarge would not have left the room on his own.

Once the two nurses were gone, Maya shared her theory that it was a crew member not a passenger who was behind the attacks.

David nodded. "I think you're probably right. If a passenger had been down in the crew area someone would have directed them to leave."

"How are the room service meals set up and delivered?"

"There is a board with room numbers up

for delivery on it," he told her. "Anyone in the kitchen would have seen that. I think the food has a room number place card with it when it's placed on a cart for delivery. Might even be sitting on the cart for a while."

"So plenty of chances to sprinkle something toxic."

"We need to talk to the woman who delivered it," David said. "She's not a suspect, but maybe she saw something."

Maya adjusted her pillow behind her back. She could feel herself getting weaker from the exertion of sitting up. "The problem is the culprit would have totally blended in. Is it only the cooks and servers who go into the kitchen area?"

"All the staff and crew have access to that kitchen. Some like to cook their own meals because of dietary restriction or preferences. It could have been a crime of opportunity. The culprit was down there, saw that we had ordered a meal and grabbed whatever poison was available."

"It has to have been something that didn't alter the flavor of the food much. Nothing tasted off to me," she said.

"You hadn't had that dish before. It did taste different to me."

David's skin was pale, and his eyes didn't

seem to have much life in them. "Are you feeling as tired as I am?"

He nodded. "I heard you talking about Sarge. I'll wait with you until we get some news."

She smiled despite herself. His desire to be supportive of her despite his weakened state touched her deeply. They continued to talk about the case as both their voices faded and the response time grew longer. Despite her concern for Sarge's welfare, the heaviness of sleep took over and she nodded off. Hours later she awoke in the darkness. David snored faintly.

Where was Sarge? Where was her partner?

The sound of voices at the far end of the room forced David to climb out of his deep slumber. In the dim light, he could just make out Maya in her hospital bed. The IV allowed her to sleep only on her back. Her hands rested on top of each other over her heart.

Footsteps came toward them.

Maya stirred awake lifting her head. "Who is it?" Fear permeated her voice.

"Not sure." Maybe her fear made sense. They were both in no condition to fend off any kind of an attack. He wouldn't put it past the assailant to take advantage of their weakened state and the lack of security around them.

He tuned his ears to the sounds around him. At least two sets of footsteps were coming toward them. Maybe that was a good sign.

A curtain was pulled back. John, the male nurse, stuck his head in. "Maya, I have a surprise for you."

She struggled to push herself into a sitting position. The curtain was pulled back even more revealing Noah and Sarge. The dog wagged his tail and whined.

Maya let out a cry of joy.

"It's against regulations to let a dog in here, but I thought we could let it slide for just a minute," John said.

Maya looked at Noah. "What happened? How did Sarge end up with you?"

The dog wouldn't stop wagging his tail and whining but he remained beside Noah.

"Just as I was getting off shift, I saw the call on the board that was from David's room number. You guys had already been transported. I went to the room and found your dog just sitting there waiting. When I called in to the infirmary, they said they would let me know when you two were out of the woods and awake."

"Someone else must have taken the call," John mused.

"Anyway, Sarge has been good company," Noah said. "He mostly slept at the foot my bed while I tried to get some shut-eye. Would have been here sooner, but I only woke up a bit ago."

Maya directed her question to the nurse. "Can he come over and say hello to me?"

"Sure," John replied.

Maya commanded Sarge to come over to the side of her bed that was opposite of where the IV was. The dog stood up and put his paws up on the bed and Maya leaned forward so she could get some doggie kisses. "I missed you."

David felt a sense of joy at witnessing the reunion between the two partners.

John excused himself, saying he had another patient he needed to deal with.

Maya commanded Sarge to get down. The dog returned to Noah.

The officer leaned over and grasped the leash. "I'll watch him until you two are released."

"Hopefully, that will be in a few hours. We really can't afford to stay here much longer." The one thing that was clear to David was that Noah could be taken off the suspect list. He had had an opportunity to take Sarge out of the picture and instead had made sure the dog was taken care of.

David signaled for Noah to come closer. He spoke in a low tone. "I need you to go back on duty. See if you can track down the woman who delivered our meal. Her name's Angie."

"I know Angie."

"Then if you can talk to the kitchen staff that was on duty when our meal was prepared, see if anyone saw anything unusual, if there's anything poisonous that is missing and if anyone acts suspicious when you question them. I'm not sure what would be in a kitchen that could poison someone so quickly. Cleaning products maybe."

"Got it. You two take care of yourselves." He left with the dog in tow.

Maya let out a heavy breath. "I wish Sarge could stay here with me."

"Why don't we both get a few hours' rest and then get out of here and see if we can track down our poisoner."

"I agree. We can't waste any more time. The killer is out there, and I have a feeling he is going to escalate as we get closer to catching him."

EIGHT

After getting a few hours' rest in the infirmary, Maya and David were released. They agreed that trying to work through the night with most everything shut down would be pointless though both of them were anxious to track down the poisoner.

They returned to their respective rooms to get more sleep so they could start the morning stronger and feeling more like themselves. Her stomach and throat still felt raw. She was going to have to eat very bland food for a while. At her request, Noah brought Sarge back to Maya's room.

Once the security officer identified himself, she opened the door. Feeling a rush of affection, she gathered Sarge in her arms. "There's my good buddy." She leaned back and stroked his soft head. "I missed you." Sarge wagged his tail and leaned into her petting.

"He's a good guy," Noah said.

She stood up and held a hand out to him. "Thank you for taking care of Sarge."

"No problem."

At least Noah was the one green-eyed crew member they could cross off the suspect list. "Were you able to track down the woman who delivered our food?"

"Yes. Angie said she didn't see anything out of the ordinary. I questioned the rest of the crew who were on shift at the time your meal was being prepared, and all of them gave the same report."

"So a dead end." Still, it helped to know that they weren't looking at passengers as suspects at this point.

She said good-night to Noah and closed the door making sure it was locked and dead bolted. Maya crawled into bed and invited Sarge up as well. Normally, the dog slept on the floor, but she'd missed him and the scare over harm coming to her partner made her want to be close to him.

Sarge snuggled in at the foot of the bed.

After taking the sleeping pill the infirmary had given her, Maya stared at the ceiling. Her mind raced with all that had happened. She'd have to at least text Lorenza about the poisoning and being able to narrow the suspect down to crew members. She wondered how things were going with the other cases the unit was dealing with. It wasn't just the missing bride/wedding party murder investigation that was on the docket. There were two other much more personal cases. Eli Partridge the tech guru who helped the unit out was desperately trying to find his godmother's survivalist family before it was too late. His godmother had cancer and her only wish was to see her son and his family.

Maya rolled over on her side hoping the sleeping pill would kick in soon.

The other investigation that was very personal for the whole unit concerned Lorenza's assistant Katie whose aunt ran the family reindeer ranch, which had experienced the theft of some of their stock as well as someone opening a pen and letting reindeer out.

Hopefully, she would be back on shore and ready to help out soon enough. She closed her eyes, as her muscles grew heavy and she fell asleep.

She slept through the night until she heard David's soft tapping on the door between their rooms.

"You up?"

"I'm awake but not ready."

"Look, I've got a security situation that requires my attention. Once you're ready, call me or get Hans to escort you. Text me and I'll let you know where I'm at on the ship."

"Okay." Though she felt groggy from the sleeping pill, she sat up. David still seemed to keep military hours. He must not have taken the sleeping aid.

Maya got up, showered and dressed. When she texted David, he said he would meet her in ten minutes at her door. She read her Bible and waited.

Ten minutes later, a text popped up on her phone.

I'm here.

She hurried toward the door, slid back the dead bolt and prepared to turn the knob. But then a thought occurred to her. How hard would it be for the attacker to steal David's phone or somehow make it look like the text had come from his phone?

She rested her palm against the door. "David, I need to hear your voice."

"Maya, it's me." Even with the barrier of the door between them, his voice sounded strong. His voice possessed a warmth that made her feel inexplicably drawn to him.

She opened the door. David smiled, making his blue eyes light up. Maybe she was reading into things, but something about him seemed different. With all they had been through together, she was starting to feel a deep bond toward him. She couldn't quite sort her feelings out. Especially since David had walls around his heart no one could climb over or break down, and he'd made it clear that he was a confirmed bachelor.

"I'm not sure where to start today with figuring out who is behind this," he admitted.

"I assume all staff and crew have photo IDs, right?"

"Yes, the IDs allow different crew members access to different parts of the ship. Just like a driver's license it lists eye color and all of them would be on file." David confirmed. As the two of them discussed their next move, they walked side by side through the corridor. "Green is not the most common eye color, but we are talking a lot of guys to call in for questioning. We'd have to sort through the IDs by hand, though, because I don't have software that would do that."

As they stood by the elevator waiting for it to arrive, his blue eyes locked on hers. Her breath caught in her throat. What was going on here?

The doors opened, and they stepped inside. "I suppose we could head to the security office and at least get an estimate of how many suspects we'd be looking at."

Maya was trying to concentrate on the case, but she couldn't let go of why her heart was fluttering every time David looked at her. Sarge, who had taken up a position between them, seemed to pick up on her change in mood. The dog shifted his weight and then lifted his chin and made a noise that was between a moan and a growl.

David gazed down at Sarge and the elevator rose up another floor. "What's up with him?"

"He's just asking me a question."

"About what?"

Her cheeks felt suddenly flushed. She stared at the wall. "David, do you suppose you'd ever consider having a home that wasn't moving?"

"This job suits me. I don't like the idea of being settled anywhere." The doors slid open. "Why do you ask?" He stood aside so she could leave first.

She noted the probing intensity in his expression when she looked at him. "Just trying to get to know you better. Even with all that has happened, working this case with you has been good." She stepped out with Sarge heeling beside her. Well, that was that. The little spark she felt began to wane. They were two very different people with incompatible ideas about what a good life looked like.

David moved to walk beside her. "You don't think you'd ever like living on a ship?"

With his question, her feelings swung back toward attraction. "The ship has been fun… in the short term even with the investigation putting me in peril. I'm kind of a homebody though. Besides, Sarge needs a place to run and train." His question made her wonder if maybe he was having some of the same feelings as she was. Hard to tell with this man, though.

David's radio made a crackling noise. He pulled it off his belt and pressed the talk button. "Yes."

"Missing child from the play area. Mom just called it in two minutes ago. Female three years old. Wearing yellow pants and a matching top."

The voice was not Noah's. It must be a different security officer.

"On it." David broke into a run.

She and Sarge kept pace with him as they hurried to the deck where the play area was. Once they arrived there, it wasn't hard to spot who the mom of the missing child was. The stricken expression on her face told Maya this was the woman.

There were people milling around the play equipment looking in nooks and crannies. A blond man in a security uniform hurried toward them.

"Hans what can you tell me?" David asked.

"We've locked down this deck, so no one can leave. The play area has been searched pretty thoroughly. I think the kid wandered off...or..."

Hans didn't say what everyone feared. That the child had been abducted. Maya assumed if that became the presumed theory, hiding the little girl would be hard given that they could probably lock the whole ship down and room-to-room searches would have to be conducted. She hoped it didn't come to that. Then another thought occurred to her, an even worse scenario but one that was more likely on a ship. What if the little girl had fallen overboard?

David scanned the play area and the shops beyond. "Obviously, we need to widen the search."

"Some volunteers have already started to spread out," Hans told him. "We've got an alert sent out. Any shop owners or passengers who see her will let us know right away."

"Lot of area to cover," David said. "Let's go." He took off at a jog, then looked back over his shoulder at her.

Maya waved indicating he should keep going. She'd be safe, Sarge was with her and there were plenty of people around.

She looked toward the mom who was clutching a stuffed animal to her chest. Maybe her K-9 partner could help out. Sarge was not a trained tracking dog but if he could follow the scent of a weapon, he might be able to pick up on that of a little girl.

Maya ran over to the mom. "Is that your daughter's?"

The woman didn't answer, but the teenage girl standing beside her did. "Yes, it belongs to my little sister Bess. We found it over there." The teen pointed toward a slide.

"If we could borrow the toy, my dog might be able to pick up the trail of where your sister went."

The teen nodded and lifted the stuffed animal out of the dazed mother's hands.

"Find my little girl. Find my baby."

"We'll do our best." Maya hoped her words communicated some degree of reassurance. She bent down and waved the toy in front of Sarge's nose. The dog's ear perked up, but then he sat back down on his haunches. Fighting off the disappointment, Maya kneeled so she was at Sarge's level. She wasn't going to give up that easily. Again, she lifted the toy to Sarge's nose. "Come on, buddy. Do this for me." She gave him the same command she used when he was tracking the scent of a weapon. "Find."

Sarge stood up. He wagged his tail as if asking her a question. She nodded and stroked his head. "You can do this."

Sarge stepped side to side and then put his nose to the ground. He took off toward the playground equipment ending up at the slide where the toy had been dropped and the little girl had last been seen. Sarge had the scent of the missing girl.

The dog yanked on the leash as he left the play area. Maya sprinted to keep up with him. The scent was probably fresh enough that it was still strong and distinctive. Sarge veered away from the main thoroughfare of shops and eateries down a side corridor, behind the establishments, where the employees entered and probably received deliveries to restock inventory when the ship was in port.

The dog doubled back and shot down a side corridor running even faster. Then he stopped and alerted beside a door. The sign indicated that this was the back entrance to a French bistro.

Maya glanced up and down the corridor not sure why Sarge had stopped. Praying he hadn't lost the scent, she was about to open the door to the back side of the café when she heard an odd squeaking sound. Sarge let out a single yipping bark.

He tugged on the leash. Straining toward the noise, they turned down yet another hallway. Up ahead a woman pushed a cart stacked with fresh folded table linens. The bottom of the cart was concealed by a fabric skirt.

Sarge jerked on the leash and yipped again. The woman pushing the cart craned her head to look back at them.

"Could you wait up for just a second!" Maya jogged toward the linen cart while Sarge heeled beside her.

The Malinois shifted his weight side to side.

"Your dog seems upset," the woman said.

"Just excited," Maya explained. She lifted the fabric skirt and let out a huge sigh of relief. It was Bess. The little girl, all dressed in yellow, was asleep on the folded linens. Curly brown hair surrounded a round pink-cheeked face, and the child sucked on two fingers while she slept. Maya straightened up and spoke in a whisper. "You've been hauling a sleeping toddler around."

"What?"

"You must have had the linen cart close to the playground at some point."

"Yes, I parked it there while I went in to talk

to a friend who runs one of the nearby shops."
The woman looked a little guilty.

"No harm done. She must have crawled on
when no one was looking." Maya lifted her
head, searching for a sign or direction arrows
that might tell her where she was. "If you could
just tell me what this part of the ship is called."

"This is the east corridor hallway deck four."

Maya pulled out her phone and texted David.

Toddler has been found. Bring her mom. She
texted the location.

Bess made a moaning sound and started to
stir. Maya feared if the little girl woke up and
saw only strangers she might be scared. All
her concerns were allayed when she heard a
sweet voice say, "Doggie."

Leave it to Sarge to break the ice. He wagged
his tail but looked to Maya for permission to
move. Bess poked her head out. When she
looked at Maya her forehead crinkled. Her
gaze wandered to the hallway and the feet of
the woman who had pushed the cart.

"Bess, your mom will be here in just a minute. May I help you get out of there?"

The toddler nodded.

Maya reached in and pulled Bess out, setting
her on her feet. The little girl took her fingers
out of her mouth and pointed again at Sarge.

"You can pet him."

Bess giggled as she stroked Sarge's head. The dog leaned into the child's touch clearly enjoying the attention.

Footsteps muffled by carpet rushed up the corridor. Bess's mother ran toward them and swept the toddler up into her arms. She was laughing and crying at the same time as she held her child close.

David had been right behind the mom. Bess's sister followed, rushing toward mother and child.

"You scared all of us kiddo," the sister said.

After thanking Maya several times, the family headed down the hallway. The mom held Bess and Bess's sister patted her sibling's curly head as they disappeared around the corner.

"I'm glad everything turned out okay. Happy endings are always the best," murmured the woman pushing the linen cart. "I have to get back to work."

David's expression's glowed with affection as he looked toward Maya. "Good job."

"It was mostly Sarge's nose and instinct. He's always had a connection with kids." Again, when he looked at her, she felt that heart flutter.

"Maybe someday, you'll be married and Sarge will have some kids to watch over."

"I wouldn't count on it," she said. "Dating

and being a K-9 officer don't seem terribly compatible."

"You never know."

She wondered why he was bringing up kids and marriage. As they stood there alone in the hallway and she felt the jolt of attraction between them, she had to remind herself not to read into the conversation. David had told her flat out that he was not interested in any kind of settled life.

"Are you hungry?" he asked.

"Starving."

"Let's go down to the crew kitchen. We're going to have to cook our own meals from now on. Or eat things sealed in packages."

"That seems like a reasonable precaution," she agreed. "Maybe we can kind of casually ask around while we are making breakfast. I know Noah asked some questions of the crew that was on duty last night, but it never hurts to probe people's memories."

David fell in step with her. "Sounds good. We can poke around and see if we can find any possible sources for the poison although I suspect that if there was anything left of what was used, it's been tossed overboard."

"It's just a little two easy to get rid of evidence on a ship, isn't it?" She said.

"Yes, and bodies too. Not trying to be morbid. But in some ways a ship is a perfect place to commit a crime."

She kept pace with him. "Except that the culprit is trapped on the ship."

"Until we get into port."

As they made their way through the ship to the crew kitchen, Maya felt a tension in her muscles. They had to find the murderer. The clock was ticking.

By the time David and Maya entered the crew kitchen after leaving Sarge in the room, the early morning rush was over. His stomach growled. There were only a few stragglers and one chef cleaning up. Most of the people still in the kitchen probably had the day off or worked night shifts and could afford to have a late breakfast.

He turned toward Maya. "What do you feel like eating?"

Her face blanched. "What would be the safest?"

She must be remembering the trauma of the poisoning. "The safest would be dry granola bars, but I think if I make pancakes from scratch, we should be fine. The place is not crowded. Chef is just finishing up. We'll be the only ones in the kitchen so we can keep an eye on everything."

"Great, and I'll scramble some eggs."

He fired up one of the griddles while she searched one of the industrial-sized refrigerators. She returned with eggs and milk. He went to the pantry to retrieve the flour and baking soda. On his way, he flung open a cupboard where he knew cleaning supplies were stored. It seemed a futile activity to try to figure out what had been used to poison them. Once they could get the samples to a lab, maybe they would reveal something about the killer, but for now it seemed the best choice would be to try to narrow down the suspects.

He returned to where Maya was waiting for him.

"I got the eggs mixed up in a bowl. But I didn't want to pour them on the grill until the pancakes were close to being done. That way everything will be warm and yummy."

Maybe it was something about seeing Maya with Bess that had made him imagine pictures of domestic bliss in his head. She was just so different from any of the other women he'd dated. Yet although he felt drawn to her in that moment, he had to remind himself that he had a lousy track record where women were concerned...

More conflicted thoughts flitted through his mind as they worked side by side. He mixed pancakes and poured them on the grill, watching them closely for the bubbling that indicated he needed to flip them. Their shoulders touched as she spread the eggs onto the griddle and scrambled them with a spatula.

"It smells good," she said.

Though he still felt that same spark between them now, he knew he had to let go of the idea that there could be anything but a friendship between as much as he enjoyed this time with her. Even a friendship would be strained by how often he was away at sea.

They finished cooking. David fished out some syrup that had not been opened as well as individual containers of orange juice that were sealed with a foil cover. All of the precautions reminded him that the killer was out there waiting for another chance to get at Maya and Sarge and that he didn't mind taking David out as collateral damage.

When they sat down to eat, only one other person remained in the kitchen, an older woman in a maid's uniform.

They bowed their heads while David thanked God for the food.

Maya stared down at her plate. "This looks so good. That was fun to cook together."

The warmth and affection that permeated

her voice was a reminder that he needed to nip this in the bud.

"As work colleagues, Maya, I enjoy your company." His words held a chilly quality on purpose.

Her features hardened. "Yes, David. It has been good to work with you and spend time together." Her voice had turned cold as well.

Just as long as she understood the boundary. He didn't want to hurt her or lead her on. Even if he did feel a special connection to her, they were two people from two different worlds. He couldn't fathom how those worlds would ever fit together.

NINE

Maya found herself grateful when their meal was interrupted by a text from the K-9 unit's forensic scientist, Tala Ekho. Whatever blossoming feelings she harbored for David, he had made it clear that he wasn't interested. Focusing on her work would take her mind off the disappointment she was experiencing. She reread the text.

We've had some developments in the wedding party murder. Call when you can. Want to keep you in the loop.

She looked up from her phone. "I have to make a ship to shore call. It would be nice if I could have consistent Wi-Fi, which I've noticed we don't get down here."

David finished up his last bite of breakfast. "Your better choice would be the internet café on deck six. I can escort you there."

"Sounds good. Let's pick up Sarge from the room on the way." Even as they spoke, Maya felt David's walls going up all around him. She'd breached some emotional boundary by expressing affection for him. She sensed though that it wasn't meanness that had made him become all brusque and businesslike, it was *fear*. And even though David had been crystal clear about where they stood, she found herself wanting to know more about why he'd shut her down so quickly. Was it just the incompatibility of their lives...or something deeper?

They loaded their dishes in the mostly full dishwasher and stopped back at her cabin room to get Sarge. As they walked down the labyrinth of the hallways, she told herself she needed to let go of her curiosity about David and focus on what mattered the most. Her work with the Alaskan K-9 unit. They headed up to the internet café, and once they arrived, the attendant provided her with log-on information so she could set up a video call.

While she sat waiting for the call to go through, David cupped his hand on her shoulder. "I'm technically on duty as of ten minutes ago. If I get called away, please wait here until I can come get you or send one of the other security officers."

She was surprised he had gone back to work

so quickly. She still felt weak from the poisoning. But then again, wasn't that what she was doing too by getting briefed on the wedding party investigation? Maybe, like her, David had had no choice but to jump back into the fray. She hoped for both their sakes it was a quiet day.

Tala's face came up on the video screen. Her long dark hair was pulled back in a ponytail, and the round silver-framed glasses she wore seemed to make her brown eyes even darker and more intense. "Maya, so good to see you."

Tala worked out of Anchorage at the state crime lab. She handled most of the evidence pertaining to the K-9 unit's cases. Seeing anyone connected to her job tugged at Maya's heart. Especially after David's rejection. She missed being on land and working side by side with the team.

"Hey, Tala, what's up?"

"Lorenza wanted to make sure you were up-to-date on any breakthroughs with the cases we're working on," the other woman said. "We've had a big surprise with the wedding party murders."

"Oh really! Did they catch Violet James? Lorenza said they thought she'd been spotted in Anchorage."

"I don't know about that. You'd have to talk

to Eli," Tala replied. "He was going to look at footage from where she was spotted."

Maya made a mental note that calling Eli Partridge, the tech guru who helped the team out, might be the next order of business. "So what's the development?"

"As you know, the groom and the best man have said all along that it was the bride, Violet James, who killed the guide and pushed the bridesmaid off the cliff, which made sense considering she seems to have gone into hiding."

"Her behavior would suggest guilt, yes," Maya concurred. "Even though the bridesmaid says it's totally out of character for Violet."

"Well, now that the best man and the groom are missing, Eli is trying to track them via credit card use."

"I hope he hits pay dirt soon."

"You and me both," Tala said. "So anyway, back to my big news. You remember how the groom Lance Wells and best man Jared Dennis claimed that when they were attacked in the hospital while a guard was posted outside their room, that the perpetrator was Violet?"

"Yeah… And I recall that the reason they were attacked in the first place was because the bride coldcocked the guard, granting her access to the room." Maya furrowed her brow. "Why? Wasn't that how it all went down?"

"Not exactly. As it turns out, the guard never saw his attacker because the cameras in that hallway were disabled. The last recorded image is of someone in surgical scrubs and a face mask, an easy enough disguise to pull off in a hospital, so we couldn't ID anyone. However, there were some microscopic samples on the guard's uniform. Some hair and fibers that didn't match the guard's. The DNA matches the groom's."

Maya sat back in her chair. "Wow! This shifts the whole case. You know I had a gut feeling about the groom. There has been something fishy about Lance from the beginning, as well as his best man. How did you come up with a DNA match anyway? We checked Lance out when the murder of the guide first happened. He doesn't have a criminal record."

"That was one of the reasons it took me so long to match the samples. Violet and Lance gave each other an engagement gift of an ancestry test. Ariel was the one who told me about it. She still maintains Violet's innocence by the way."

"But if the bride hasn't done something, why doesn't she come out of hiding?" Maya's attention was drawn to David who had been pacing at the open entrance to the internet café. He was now talking on his radio, probably getting a call on something he needed to deal with.

"Motive is for the K-9 team to figure out. I just look at things under a microscope. Speaking of which, I need to get back to work."

Maya stared at the screen. "Thanks for the update. It was good to see you, Tala."

She hung up and the screen went black. When she looked over at the entrance to the internet café, David was gone.

That meant she was stuck here until David could come back or she would have to summon one of the other security officers. A wave of nausea suddenly roiled through her. Great. Her stomach felt like it was in even more turmoil than before.

To make matters worse, she was the only one in the internet café besides the attendant. Sarge lay at her feet. "I don't suppose you have anything on hand for an upset stomach?"

The attendant who looked like he was barely out of his teens looked up from his laptop and stared at her for a moment. She realized it was a bizarre question to ask someone who ran an internet café, but she would not be able to leave the café as per David's orders. Maybe the clerk had been sick at one time and had something around.

"No, there's a pharmacy down the first hallway to your right," he said.

She had a vague memory of having seen a

sign with an arrow for it when she and David had come toward the internet café.

Her stomach churned again. She feared she was going to be sick. Had she been poisoned again? She stood up and tugged on Sarge's leash, glad that he was with her. This part of the ship was not a place with heavy passenger traffic. She saw only one other person walking away from her up the long corridor. As she read the signs on the doors, it looked like it consisted of places people would seek out because of particular needs. She passed a lost and found and also saw a sign indicating the infirmary was on this floor, which helped her orient herself a little. Her entrance and exit from the infirmary the previous night had been kind of a blur.

Maya followed the sign to the pharmacy. An older man was behind the counter. She found the shelf that contained medicine for stomach upset and selected a bottle. After paying the clerk, she texted David that she had left the internet café to go to the pharmacy but would head back there now. She didn't want him to return and worry that something had happened to her.

When she didn't get a text right back, she assumed he must still be out dealing with whatever the radio call had been about.

The pharmacy did have a public bathroom

which she used to take some of the medicine she had just purchased. Afterward, Maya took the short walk up the hallway toward the internet café. She saw no one which gave her an uneasy feeling. Back at the café, the doors were still open, but the young clerk had disappeared. Maybe he was in the back room.

She checked her phone, but David had not texted her back.

She typed in another message.

Clerk is gone. Here by myself. Feeling a little vulnerable without you.

Her finger hovered over the send button. Sending such a text meant she was admitting something to David. She was a trained police officer with a K-9 partner who had her back, and yet she felt the safest when David was close by.

Maya pressed Send and sat back in her chair. She looked at the laptop in front of her thinking she should use the time to get in touch with the tech guru, Eli Partridge, to find out if he had made any headway in tracking down the missing groom and best man or in locating the bride. Her stomach was still doing a gymnastic routine while her hand hovered over the keyboard.

Then she heard approaching footsteps out in the corridor.

* * *

David hurried to deck eight where the call about an altercation had come in. This part of the ship had several hot tubs beneath a glass ceiling and a shuffleboard court and a virtual putting green. Several senior citizens were engaged in the shuffleboard game and he spotted four people in one of the hot tubs. Everyone appeared very relaxed.

His throat went tight. The call had come in as an emergency.

One older man playing shuffleboard looked in his direction. "Everything all right?"

David shook his head and turned to run in the direction he'd just come. "Just fine." He'd been set up, lured away from Maya.

As he increased his pace from a jog to a sprint, pain shot through his injured leg. He swung the door to the stairs open and hurried down. Once on the deck where Maya was, he ran as fast as he could to the internet café. When he got there, Sarge sat up in an alert stance. His tail thumped when he saw David. The clerk was behind the counter staring at his laptop. He looked up when David stepped into the café.

"The woman who was here?"

The attendant shrugged. "I went in the back to deal with some inventory. She left to go get something for her stomach." He pointed at the dog. "She must have come back while I was in the back room and then left her dog behind."

David's mind reeled. Was it possible the killer had managed to abduct or subdue her with Sarge so close?

"Did you see anyone else?"

The clerk closed his laptop. "Actually, I did. A guy came by twice and peered in like he was looking for something or someone. When I asked him if he needed help, he just shrugged."

"What did he look like?"

"I don't know. Average build, brown hair."

Pushing down a rising panic, David turned one way and then the other. "How long ago was that?"

"Five to seven minutes."

David could not piece together what had happened. The guy would not have come back looking for Maya if he already had her. Sarge was alert but not agitated. He looked at the dog. "Where did she go?"

Sarge wandered over to him and licked his hand.

"Hey." The voice behind him was more welcoming than a cool breeze on a hot day.

He whirled around to see Maya. She was extremely pale and clutching her stomach.

Joy surged through him. Even though she

did not look well, he was glad she had not been harmed. "You okay?"

"Not really, I got sick and had to run to the bathroom. I don't think I am fully recovered yet from the poisoning."

"Oh no, so sorry to hear that." David took a step toward her. "When you weren't here, I was a little afraid something might have happened. The call I went on was a false alarm."

Her hand fluttered from her stomach to her neck. "Do you think our suspect made the call to lure you away, so I'd be alone?"

"Yes, and the clerk said a man came by here twice and looked in."

"Let me guess." She blew out an agitated breath. "He was of medium build, totally generic in appearance and too far away to notice if he had green eyes."

He hadn't asked the clerk if he'd noticed eye color, but since the young man hadn't mentioned something that distinctive, Maya was probably right. The near miss with the attacker was a reminder of how vulnerable she was. If she hadn't gone to the bathroom, if the timing of the clerk being in a back room had been different, David might not be looking into her beautiful brown eyes right now. "Glad you're okay. I was really worried."

"I did send you two texts."

He pulled his phone out. "There was no time to check them. I thought the most important thing was to ensure that you were not in danger." He looked at both texts. The first one was straightforward, just saying she had gone to the pharmacy on the same deck. However, the second caused a tightening in his throat. *Feeling a little vulnerable without you.* It was almost like she was admitting that she liked having him around. Maya could obviously take care of herself—as a highly skilled state trooper he figured she had all kinds of self-defense training. But did she feel safer when he was close? When he looked up from his phone, she stared at the floor as though self-conscious.

Against his will, his own face felt flushed. He smiled and shook his head. Despite how he tried to keep his defenses up, she had a way of getting to him. "It's nice to know you feel that way."

Her expression was glowing. Sarge, standing by her feet, wagged his tail.

He could at least admit that he felt an attraction to Maya. Even if nothing could come of it. He needed to keep reminding himself, and her, of that. His voice took on a businesslike quality. "I have some regular check-ins and follow-ups I need to do with some of the establishments that reported crimes. We have a bit of an employee theft problem in one of the shops. I need to pick up their surveillance footage. You and Sarge can come along with me."

The brightness faded from her features. "Sure, David. I need to make another ship to shore call to Eli Partridge sometime today—he's the tech wiz that works with the K-9 Unit."

"Some of the stuff I have to do is time sensitive." He stepped outside of the café and Maya fell in beside him. "We can work in the video chat when things are slower or maybe when I get off shift. I don't want you down here alone though."

"Sure, I get that. But I need to stay abreast of the unit's current investigations. Maybe we can come down here on your break or something."

"We'll work something out."

The whole conversation seemed stiff. Like they were both trying to avoid talking about their feelings by focusing on their respective jobs. Maybe they'd both crossed a line and the start of what might have been a unique friendship had become uncomfortable.

"Are you free to speak about the cases the team is working on? I might be able to provide some input. Sometimes just talking a case out can make light bulbs go on."

"You're right about that. It's hard not to be part of the investigation. Especially, the one involving a wedding party homicide. I was very involved when the case first broke."

"Tell me about it?"

She had a moment's hesitation about discussing the cases. "I would love to troubleshoot with you about them. But let me message my boss and ask permission first." She sent the text. "If she doesn't get back to me...as much as I would like to, I really shouldn't."

The fact the Maya respected the ethics of police work made him like her only more. Her phone dinged a few seconds later. She read the text. "My boss says it's okay to talk to you about the investigations."

As she shared the details of the case, the tension between them seemed to dissolve. He felt more comfortable when they kept their conversation work focused. And he did enjoy helping her as much as he liked it when she and Sarge assisted him.

However, as they made their way through the corridors and up to the next deck, he realized that her expressing her feelings in the text and the awareness that the same feelings were growing in him made him very uneasy.

TEN

Maya sat in the security office looking at all the employee records as well as copies of their IDs in the computer database. There was no way she would have the time to isolate the green-eyed crew members without sorting software. They had to find a way to narrow down the suspects even more. The attacks and the murder had taken place in different parts of the ship. Which meant they were dealing with someone who not only knew the layout of the ship but also could pinpoint the most isolated areas to find a woman alone, and at what time.

The question that rose to the surface for her was that if they were looking at someone who had been with the cruise line long term, there must be an inciting incident that triggered him to start trying to kill women and to have succeeded once.

Sarge relaxed at her feet while David sat in the chair next to her looking on a separate screen at surveillance videos from the store that was experiencing employee theft. The handsome security chief looked bored to death as he rested his chin in his palm and watched the screen. She noticed a little scar by his eyebrow and wondered what the story was behind it. A childhood accident or was it from the injury that had stolen his army career from him?

Though they seemed to stumble from one awkward moment to the next, she still found herself wanting to know more about him. Sharing with him about the wedding party investigation had eased the angst she felt at not being on land working the case with the rest of the K-9 team. She scooted her chair and leaned sideways so she had a view of David's screen. Not much happening; a customer moved around the store and the clerk remained behind the counter. "Like watching paint dry, huh?"

He clicked the pause button. "Not quite as exciting. How about you?"

"I'm wondering if you can pull up the crime reports from shortly before the murder took place. That would have been right before the cruise left Seattle or maybe a few days before. I don't know where the file is, and I assume it's password protected."

David pointed at her computer. "I can pull it up for you."

She scooted over to give him access to her computer. His fingers clicked on the keyboard. "Here, this is three days prior to the murder."

They both leaned forward to see the screen better, their heads nearly touching. He scrolled through the number of reported incidents, which averaged only about five per day. Mostly petty theft, minor injury and public intoxication, nothing overly violent. No report of a fight between a man and woman or between two men brawling over a woman, which was what she would be looking for. A man who had just been dumped or betrayed might seek revenge on another women if he was psychologically unbalanced. Some of the things the attacker had said to her made her believe that was true.

She shook her head. "No red flags there." She and David were huddled so close together that when she turned her head toward him, she could smell the soapy cleanness of his skin. The proximity caused heart flutters for her.

"I hate to say it. But I think we are going down a rabbit trail that won't open up any leads for us." David scooted away a few inches and turned his attention back to the screen where he had paused the surveillance footage of the store.

He was right. Her jaw clenched in frustration.

"I've had to look at surveillance footage for my job too. Maybe I could help you," she offered.

"Sure, a second set of eyes might help. We think the thefts are occurring during store hours, not when the store is closed. A quick skim through of the after-hours surveillance didn't show any movement."

He restarted the footage he'd been viewing and then reached over and handed her a disk. "This is for a different day. You can watch it on your computer."

After a few hours of watching footage that revealed nothing, Maya thought she might fall asleep. "Why don't we take Sarge to do his business and grab a coffee or I'm going to need a nap."

David chuckled. "Ah, the glamorous world of on-board security."

"I get it. Not all police work is exciting." She found herself enjoying his company even when they were doing the most tedious thing in the world.

David locked up the security office and they headed out to the play area for Sarge after getting coffee. They sipped their coffee and watched Sarge and one other dog play. The ship was alive and bustling with midday activity. Passengers heading toward recreational areas of the ship, or eating or shopping or visiting in the botanical gardens.

She smiled as a group of giggling preteen girls ran by. "It's like a little floating city."

"You could say that." He took a sip of his coffee. "Why don't we head back to the internet café so you can make that call. Looks like work is going to be quiet for now anyway."

David mentioning the call she wanted to make to Eli reminded her that sooner or later, she was going to have to check in with Lorenza and let her know what progress they had made in the shipboard case.

She took a sip of her coffee. "Might as well. You can listen in on the call since you have a gist of the investigation."

"I'd like that, Maya."

The way he said her name warmed her to the bone. Mentally, she kicked herself. Though she could not control her involuntary responses to having him close, she knew she had to let go of the idea that there could be anything between them.

"I know your job makes it hard to have a relationship, but you could date someone else who worked on the ship." She had to know why he was so opposed to anything romantic before she gave up completely on him.

"It's just that. I have a rotten track record with women. I do all right until things get serious." He sighed. "Sometimes you can't escape the things you learned from childhood even if God is a part of your life. My father was not a good guy. I'm afraid I might end up being just like him. I haven't treated women the way he treated my mom, but like I said, I always back out when it gets serious because of that fear." David's voice was raw with emotion.

She wasn't sure what to say.

He broke the silence. "Let's go make that call." He'd purged his voice of all the intensity from the moment before speaking in a monotone.

Whatever vulnerability he'd shown was gone, and he didn't seem to understand how his coldness affected her.

Maya knew she had to let her budding feelings of attraction go. David had made up his mind about what his life was going to look like, and it didn't include a relationship with her or anyone for that matter. She felt a deep sadness for him.

She glanced at Sarge and then drew her attention upward.

They were standing in the same place where the giant pot had been pushed off in order to kill her. She shuddered at the memory. Except for the near miss at the internet café, the assailant hadn't come after her since the poisoning.

David stepped a little closer and followed the line of her gaze. "He's not likely to do the same thing twice."

"I know," she said.

"My biggest worry is that if he's not coming after you, he might be spending his time stalking another woman preparing to attack her."

Fear twisted inside her. David was probably right. There was more at stake than just her own safety. They had to catch this guy before they got into port.

David and Maya made their way up to the internet café. This time they weren't the only ones in the café. A middle-aged woman wearing a swimming suit cover-up and sandals sat making a video call. David showed his ID so Maya wouldn't have to pay for the time wishing he had thought to do that the first time they'd been down here. One of the perks of working on the ship. Maya had already settled in front of a laptop.

David scooted in beside her. There was something about helping the pretty law enforcement officer stay engaged with her team's investigation that eased the frustration he felt about their search for the killer on the ship.

These cases were far removed from the immediate danger that she and any other attractive woman on board faced.

Maya typed in the code that would allow her to make a ship to shore video call. She was sitting close enough to him that he could detect the floral scent of her perfume. If he was honest with himself, part of what was so appealing about helping her out was getting to be close to her. But he knew from experience that it took more than physical attraction to make a relationship work. David sighed, resolving just to enjoy this time with her and not open the door to there being anything more.

A man with a thin face and round black glasses popped up on the screen. "Hey, Maya. Good to see you."

It looked like the man was in some sort of cluttered office. There was a stack of books, file cabinets and computers in the background.

"Eli, how is it going?"

"It goes like it does. Always good to see your smiling face."

Maya tilted her head toward David. "Eli, this is security chief David Garrison. He's helping me out with the shipboard investigation. I've invited him to listen in on the progress with our cases on land. I value his input and experience."

The compliment elevated David's mood. His job could be pretty thankless and petty sometimes. He was glad Maya acknowledged his expertise.

Eli smoothed his hand over a mop of curly brown hair. "Nice to meet you, David." He turned slightly. "So let me guess, you're calling about progress with the wedding party murders?"

"Just thought I would check in with the source. Lorenza said that you might have a lead on our missing bride. Someone called in to the tip line about seeing her. You were going to look at some surveillance footage?"

"Yes, we think it is Violet James but in disguise— sunglasses and hiking hat low on her face. I had to watch the footage several times. She has some distinctive mannerisms and at one point for just a second, she looks at the camera, which means she doesn't realize it's there. She popped up again in the same area yesterday. We're not sure why she keeps going to that area of Anchorage. This is the second time we had a direct feed from that camera when she showed up. K-9 Officers Sean West and Gabriel Runyon were dispatched, but they were too late."

"I wish she'd turn herself in. Being in disguise suggests a level of guilt or wanting to hide, but why is she taking the risk and coming into town like that?"

Eli shrugged. "Who knows. To see someone she cares about? But she has no known relatives in Anchorage."

"If she'd just turn herself in, we could let her know that the groom and best man are under suspicion and missing now."

The tech guru nodded. "Exactly. It is hard to piece this together based on the way the people involved are acting. Maybe the groom, best man and bride were all involved in the murder of that guide and in pushing the bridesmaid off the cliff."

"The only one for sure we know is not involved is Ariel, and she insists Violet is innocent," Maya said. "But we can't believe her just because she's engaged to one of the K-9 officers until the evidence supports that."

David leaned closer to the screen. "So is there any more news about tracking down the groom and best man?"

"We're watching their bank accounts and credit cards. Nothing so far," Eli replied.

"Text me if there are any changes, will you?" Maya said. "I want to hit the ground running with these cases once the one on the ship gets wrapped up."

"Sure thing." It looked like Eli was eating

a snack or late lunch. He'd taken an apple out of a nearby container as well as what looked like slices of cheese.

"Eli, can I ask? How is your godmother?" She glanced at David and then looked back at the screen. "Only share if you feel comfortable."

David wasn't sure what Maya was asking about, but judging from the change in Eli's expression, the shadow that seemed to fall over his features, it was something pretty serious.

"Bettina is hanging in there through the chemo treatments, but we haven't been able to locate her son Cole and his family."

"Eli, I'm so sorry. I'm sure that weighs heavily on you knowing that the Seaver family is hiding out somewhere in the wilderness and your godmother may not have much more time."

"We'll just keep trying. What else can we do?" Eli turned sideways to glance at a stack of papers. "Look, I better get going. Work is piling up. I'll text you if there are any new developments."

"You got it," Maya said. "Stay in touch."

She clicked out of the video feed then sat back in the chair and let out a heavy breath.

"That sounds like some pretty heavy stuff Eli has been dealing with on a personal level."

"For sure. His godmother's only wish is to be reunited with her son and his wife and her grandson. They're survivalists. We think they might be hiding out in Chugach State Park. But people who choose to live off the grid like that don't want to be found and that park is so big it really is like looking for a needle in a haystack."

The waver in Maya's voice indicated how emotionally connected she was to Eli and what he was going through. Really the way she talked about the whole K-9 team sounded like they had each other's backs, not just professionally but personally too.

The last time he'd felt deeply connected to other people and part of something bigger than himself was when he'd been in the army. With the exception of a few people on the ship, he wasn't overly social. He respected the other security officers, but didn't feel close to them.

When he saw how Maya lit up when she talked to one of her coworkers, he realized something was missing in his life.

"It's past lunchtime. Do you think you could eat something?" he asked.

"My stomach is growling. Maybe something bland like chicken soup and crackers."

"I know the perfect restaurant to get that,"

David told her. "And the perfect place to eat it so we don't have to worry about an attack."

"Lead the way."

He took her up a deck to a restaurant called Almost Mom's. Maya stared at the board posted behind the counter. While the service person waited for her to choose something to eat, David stood close to her. "Everything here is made from scratch and the chicken soup is their specialty. We can get it to go."

They ordered the food. It was late afternoon, and most of the lunch rush had subsided. Only two people, a couple, sat at a table and no one but the two of them were waiting for takeout.

Once they had their lunch in a take-out bag, she turned toward him. "So where are we going?"

"You know that round ball on a crane-looking structure at the back of the ship?"

"Yes," she murmured.

"It's called the North Star and one of the perks of working on the ship is that I can go up in it anytime as long as they're not busy. It will give you a whole different view of the ship and the scenery."

"Sounds fun!"

He phoned ahead to the operator to make sure he would be there to lift them up. By the time they got to the deck where the North Star was, the sky had darkened in the distance indicating rain might be on the way.

The deck was deserted except for the North Star operator. David addressed the man. "Hey, Glen, this is Maya. I'd like to take her and her service dog up."

Glen glanced at the sky. "If the lightning gets too close, I'll have to bring you down. Should be nice viewing of the storm. Right now, it's pretty far away."

Glen walked over to his operating panel. The North Star was a pod-like structure with windows that went around the entire ball. The door slid open. David and Maya settled into the seats and he set the bag of food on the floor. "We can eat when we're elevated."

The pod door slid closed. There was a mechanical humming as the crane arm lifted them up.

Maya stared through the window while Sarge sat at her feet. "Wow."

Being able to share this experience with her made his own heart soar. The crane stopped. Their view was of the thunderstorm moving toward them from a forest across the water in the distance.

David reached down and pulled her soup and his sandwich out of the take-out bag. He handed the soup to her along with her crackers and a plastic spoon. They ate and watched as a sheet of gray indicating where the storm was moved across the landscape. The lightning and thunder were far enough away that it was not a danger to them.

Maya took several spoonsful of soup and then looked out through the window. "God is doing some beautiful work today, isn't He?"

"I do feel closer to God when I go up here. Such an exquisite world He's given us." A light rain sprayed against the window. He took a bite of his chicken sandwich. "How's your soup?"

"Really good. It reminds me of the soup my grandma used to make. Mom and I could never get it right. It needed a touch of Grandma's love."

"Has your grandma passed away?" he asked.

"No, it's just that she is still back in Puerto Rico. If I can swing it, I go back to visit her once a year."

"Why doesn't she move here?"

"The move and the cold weather would be really hard on her." She set her empty soup container down.

"That is neat that you have a close relationship."

She turned to look at him. "There isn't anyone in your family you're close to?"

His stomach clenched in response to her inquiry. He took a french fry from the cardboard container it was in and then offered her one, which she took. "Not all of us have families we like to talk about."

"David, I didn't mean to pry."

"No, you deserve to know. I've worked really hard to be a better man than my father was. And I think that I am in many ways. But it is still a struggle to have a relationship with my mom and sister. You and I are from two very different places and I don't just mean geographically." He felt like he was pushing her away with his words at the same time that he wanted more than anything to hold her in his arms.

Maya finished munching on her cracker. She stared out at the fantastic show taking place through the window. "Look, David," she said softly. "I know that the best we could hope for between us would be an infrequent friendship. All the same, I'm going to pray that you find community, a sort of replacement family, in whatever form that takes."

Until she said something, he hadn't viewed his life as lacking in any way. Maybe he did like his job because it meant he didn't have to belong to one place or person. "I never turn down someone praying for me. But I'm not unhappy living this way. It suits me. And I do have friends. We meet for a church service and give each other prayer support."

She studied him for a long moment. "I shouldn't try to dictate what your life should look like. I just know if my home was moving all the time with a rotating cast of characters, I would feel lonely is all. But like we've been saying all along, we are two very different people."

The storm in the distance intensified and drew their attention back to the window. They watched in silence as the sheet of gray moved across the water leaving a blue sky and clouds behind it.

David relished this time he had with Maya. It felt good just to sit beside her and watch the storm while rain splashed against their viewing window. Her suggestion that he might need a deeper connection to people bounced around his head. He'd always been kind of a loner and preferred it that way. But maybe he was short-changing himself.

The storm shifted direction, now it looked like it might come closer to the ship. He signaled Glen to lower them to the deck. They'd just stepped out of the pod when his radio made a static noise. David pressed the talk button.

Hans's voice came across the line. "We got

our first drunk and disorderly of the day. Neptune's Bar. Might need some back up."

"On my way," David said.

The time with Maya had been a brief reprieve. Back to real life.

ELEVEN

Maya and Sarge trotted along beside David as they headed toward wherever they needed to go. She had no idea which deck Neptune's Bar was on.

They stepped into an elevator. David's radio indicated someone was trying to reach him. He pulled it off his belt. "Yes."

"Looks like I got it de-escalated. Wasn't as bad as the bartender made it out to be."

"Okay, thanks, Hans." He took his hand off the talk button. Then addressed Maya. "It's only late afternoon. I'm sure there'll be more calls before the night is over. Since this is the last stretch of the cruise, you usually see a rise in alcohol-related incidents."

The elevator doors slid open.

"So what now?" Maya wondered if she'd been out of line in suggesting that David needed more community in his life. She had no right to think that his life needed to look

like hers. Maybe her thinking there was something lonely about the way he lived was just
her not being able to let go of the attraction
she felt toward him. She was projecting things
onto him. Like she could somehow rescue him
from a desolation he wasn't even experiencing. Ridiculous.

They walked along a corridor that led to a
solarium. "Are you getting tired of following
me around?" David asked. "I know it's a shame
to spend a cruise in a cabin that has no windows, but that would be the only other option
I would feel comfortable with."

"Yeah, I think I would rather be with you
than alone reading or watching TV."

They stepped out into the solarium with its
floor-to-ceiling windows. Though it was late
afternoon, the storm had moved closer to the
ship, darkening the sky, so it almost appeared
to be nighttime. Lightning flashed.

The four people in lounge chairs made an
awestruck noise. One of them, an older man,
jumped out of his chair as though the lightning
might hit him.

Maya stared at the sky. "I think I liked it better when the storm was farther away."

"I'm going to have to do rounds on the outdoor viewing areas and decks to make sure no
one is trying to get up close and personal with

this storm. The ship's PA system will make a general announcement. I'm sure the captain was watching and knew the storm would head in this direction even if it looked to me like we were going to miss it."

"Yes, of course the captain is the one who makes the ultimate decisions about the ship." Maya had seen the ship's captain only at a distance when she had first boarded. She'd been so tuned into David's job responsibilities she'd started to think that he was the one running the ship.

"Procedurally, we always have to check on the exposed outdoor areas, make sure everyone is safe inside. Unfortunately, I don't have time to escort you back to your room."

"Sarge and I will go with you. I would prefer it that way."

David lifted a brow. "You sure?"

"I'm way better at being active and helpful than sitting in a room staring at the ceiling."

"Let's go then," he said.

Maya felt like she was in her element as the two of them checked several of the exposed viewing areas. The announcement came over the PA system that the storm had turned severe enough that everyone needed to be inside.

David led her to the outdoor pool. The waves

hitting the ship had become intense enough that water in the pool sloshed over the sides.

She and Sarge fought to maintain balance. David on the other hand seemed to have no problem staying upright. It must be a learned skill.

"We've got one more deck to clear," he told her. "The rest of the night will be spent in the security room watching the monitors ensuring no one decides to be a daredevil until this storm is over."

Though the situation was serious, the thought of spending the night sipping hot tea or cocoa and being with David sounded appealing. Like the times she'd been on stakeouts with other members of the K-9 team. Bottom line, she liked working with David.

"Okay, let's go." she said.

As they hurried through the pool area, Maya peered back over her shoulder. No one was behind her, but there was a series of doors that led to other places. She couldn't shake the feeling that she was being watched. Still, this was not the time to search the area for the attacker. They needed to make sure all the passengers were safe from the storm.

The last deck they needed to clear was at the front of the ship on a lower level. When they got there, it looked like crew members had already removed the lounge chairs in preparation for the storm and the tumultuous waves.

"The deck wraps around." David pointed one direction and then the other. "Don't go far."

"I'll just check around the corner and come right back."

She and Sarge trotted around to the other side of the deck. No one was there. She turned back around to go rejoin David. Hit by a heavy wave, the ship tilted to one side. She fell backwards landing on her bottom and sliding across the deck. Sarge rolled and slid as well. The ship continued to be rocked by the waves. Her heart beat faster. Even though David was not far away, she realized the difficulty in moving on the deck in the storm made her vulnerable.

She reached out for Sarge's leash which she'd dropped when she fell. She saw a pair of boots. Sarge barked, but it was as if the wind picked it up and carried it away. Barely audible.

She got to her feet still unsteady from the motion of the ship. She looked into the green eyes of the masked man. The mouth hole of the mask revealed the sneer on his lips.

Fear shot through her as her heart raced.

There were half a dozen entrances to this deck. He could have taken one of them once he figured out where she and David were going and then he'd waited for the moment when she was isolated.

The man lunged toward her. She backed up toward the railing. The attacker held up a knife and swung it at Sarge which was enough intimidation to keep Sarge from advancing toward the attacker.

"That dog is in my way." His voice held a menacing tone.

A second man emerged and grabbed Sarge's leash, dragging him. The man was not wearing a mask, but he had a bandana across most of his face.

Her heart wrenched when she heard Sarge's yelps of protest as the masked man came toward her. She doubted though that the sound would carry at all. Of course, they needed Sarge out of the way to get to her. He lifted the knife in the air. Her back pressed against the railing. "This time you're going to die. No dog to protect you." He swung again aiming to swipe across her stomach.

She rolled away before the blade could find its target, but the move put her in a vulnerable position. She was still having to deal with the motion of the ship. She turned sideways against the railing. The man lunged at her a third time, the knife cutting across her shoulder and tearing her jacket but not injuring her.

A wave rocked the ship. The knife flew out of the attacker's hand.

She moved to subdue him with a blow to the neck. But he grabbed her wrist. Then he secured her other hand. His grip was like iron.

She tried to lift her leg to drive a knee into him. His hand let go of her wrist and clamped on her neck. She struggled to breathe and could feel herself growing weaker. A wave of water washed over the deck. The man's body slammed against her, but he kept his fingers pressed on her windpipe. He looked out toward the water, let go of her and stepped away. Another wave crashed against the boat. The attacker must have seen the wave coming and it could wash him overboard.

She lost her equilibrium and gasped for breath. She could feel herself being lifted up by the water. And then she was floating. She sucked in a ragged breath. She reached out. She was holding on to some part of the ship dangling in space. The ship rocked. She lost her grip. Then her body hit something solid and she saw the black dots that indicated she was about to lose consciousness.

Her last thought was that both she and Sarge were going to die.

David hurried around to the part of the deck where Maya and Sarge had gone. He'd been

delayed when he had to usher a twenty-some-
thing couple off the deck who were filming the
storm for their online travel channel. The man
and woman had clearly had a couple of drinks
and while the exchange was friendly their response in understanding the danger and heading inside had been slow.

He had assumed he would meet Maya at the
front part of the wraparound deck. The storm
was making the waves even more dangerous.
They needed to get inside. He hurried to the
side section of the deck. Fear took over when
he didn't see Maya there. He checked the first
door where she might be standing on a stair
landing waiting for him out of the storm. No
one was there. But that didn't make any sense.
Why didn't she and Sarge just come and find
him if she'd seen that no one was on that side
of the deck? He never should have been separated from her even for a short time.

Fear overtook him as he ran toward the railing. He could see the rescue boats down below
still hooked to the side of the ship. Maya had
fallen into one of them. Her body was twisted
at an unnatural angle. Was she even alive?

He raced toward the stairs. Despite how
rocky the seas were, he took the stairs two at
a time to get to the deck where the rescue boats
were attached.

The ship was still listing side to side at intense angles. When he looked out, Maya's body rolled like a rag doll. He pressed the button that opened the automatic door that gave him access to the rescue boat. Climbing out to get to her proved a challenge on the unsteady sea. David fell into the rescue boat, landing on his knees, then crawled toward Maya praying that she wasn't dead. He cradled her head in his arms and held her, checking for a pulse. She was still alive.

Her eyes fluttered open.

"David." Her voice was weak and her gaze unfocused.

"Yes, I came for you." He looked all around. "Did you fall?"

"The man with the knife…he came after me."

David clenched his jaw. Mad at himself for letting her out of his sight. "You okay?"

She nodded.

"Where is Sarge?"

She shook her head. She opened her mouth as if to explain, but no words came out.

Something was seriously wrong, but she was still in too much shock to explain.

He'd have to deal with finding Sarge second. First, he needed to get Maya to a safe place. "I got you now, Maya. You're going to be okay."

He wrapped one arm around her. "Can you get up?"

She turned her head and stared at him as though she didn't understand what he was saying. Water sprayed against the side of the ship.

"We need to get inside, Maya."

When she looked at him, it was clear the paralysis of shock had set in. He wondered too if she might have some physical injury. "Are you hurt?"

Again, her response time was slow. She shook her head. "I don't think anything is broken."

Maya bent her head. Long strands of wet hair hid her face. The rescue boat creaked. He wrapped his arm around her back, cupping her shoulder and drawing her close.

She whispered the same words over and over. He wasn't sure what she was saying until he bent his head close to her mouth.

"Thank you, David," she said several times.

He wasn't sure if he could trust her judgment about any injuries Her back might be broken. While he still held her, David drew out his radio and called for the EMTs. "Help is on the way."

Within minutes the EMTs arrived. They crawled through and strapped Maya to a rescue backboard working together to get her on the ship and placed on a gurney.

David crawled back onto the ship as well. Before they could wheel her away, she grabbed his hand and squeezed. Her eyes had cleared, which was a good sign.

"I'm worried about Sarge. This attack was mostly about getting him out of the picture. There were two men this time. I'm afraid something may have happened to my dog."

Now he understood why she'd been unable to explain before what had happened to Sarge. "I'll do what I can." David watched as they took Maya to the infirmary to be checked out. He wasn't sure where to start the search for Sarge. So, the attacker was getting some help. Including someone else in your crime was risky. It suggested a level of desperation.

He walked a little faster. The first step would be to post a missing service dog report. The ship had its own "news" channel with viewing screens posted in strategic places. Any sale at stores, or special events on the ship were highlighted as well as weather warnings, and changes in arrival times for ports of call. If Sarge was still on the ship maybe someone had seen him with his abductor.

His biggest fear though was that Sarge had simply been tossed overboard.

TWELVE

Maya watched the ceiling clip by as the EMTs wheeled her to the infirmary. At her request, they had undone the straps on the backboard. They'd taken her vitals right away, which they said were okay. The confusion and disorientation from the shock was lifting which was the most important thing. That meant she was getting better, not worse.

As she watched the designs on the ceiling and the light fixtures change, the thing foremost on her mind was Sarge. Could she even hope that he was still alive?

One of the EMTs put his head in her field of vision. "You doing okay, ma'am?"

"Better than okay." She sat up on the stretcher. If she had broken any bones it would have been obvious by now.

"Please lie back down. You've suffered a terrible shock…at the very least."

"You said it yourself. My vitals looked impressive." She jumped off the stretcher and moved from a walk to a trot.

The EMT came after her. "We need to have the doctor say you're okay."

She spoke over her shoulder as she moved into a jog. "Later. Right now, I need to talk to the head security officer, David Garrison."

Her jog turned into a sprint. She had to do everything to find Sarge. And she refused to let go of the hope that he was still alive.

She slowed a bit in her pace. She'd lost her phone in the struggle. How was she going to find David? He might be at the security office. She headed in that direction.

She passed one of the news monitors when Sarge's picture, which David must have taken when they were in the play area, came on the screen with info about a missing service dog. That had to have been David's doing. He'd gotten the word out pretty fast.

As she came to a more crowded part of the ship, she spotted Noah dressed in plain clothes. She ran toward him.

His eyes grew wide when he saw her. "Heard you had a bit of excitement."

"Can you phone David and find out where he is? I lost my phone. I need to get another one."

Noah took his phone out. "Sure, I can call him. What's the urgency?"

"Sarge is missing."

"Yeah that came across the boards. I take it you're not really a journalist?"

Now that she knew Noah could be trusted, she was fine with him knowing. "I'm a state trooper with the Alaskan K-9 Unit that works cases all over the state."

Noah nodded and then clicked the numbers on his phone screen. He addressed his comment to her while the call was being placed. "The security office can loan you a phone." Then he spoke into the phone. "Hello, David? I have Maya here."

Maya listened to the one-sided conversation and then Noah hung up. "I'm supposed to escort you to deck four where he is scouring all the public areas for Sarge. Hans and I are also going to do a deck by deck search and remain in radio contact."

"Let's go. I feel like we've lost precious time already."

She and Noah jogged through the commercial sections of the ship where the nightlife was just starting to pick up. Music spilled out of some of the venues, and she could hear dinnertime chatter as they sprinted past the restaurants. They found David on one of the enclosed decks, talking to the patrons who were resting in the lounge chairs, showing them Sarge's picture on his phone. Noah left, promising to get in contact as soon as he had any news.

Maya stood close to David when he stepped out of earshot of the lounging passengers. "Anything at all?" Her voice cracked when she asked the question.

David shook his head. "Nothing yet." His expression softened as he stepped closer to her. "How are you doing? Did you even make it to the infirmary?"

She avoided answering the question. "Sarge has to be my priority." Time was precious. The last thing she wanted to do was spend it being checked out by a doctor.

"I was hoping maybe one of the passengers had seen something. It's not that easy to deal with a dog who I'm sure was not compliant about being dragged away from you, but so far nothing. And no calls on the bulletin that went out over the ship's news feed."

Maya's vision blurred from the tears in her eyes. "David, I don't know what I would do without Sarge. Not only is he my work partner, he's my best buddy."

"I know how connected you and that dog are. We'll pull out all the stops to find him." David squeezed her shoulder. She knew he smiled to offer reassurance, but she saw fear behind his eyes.

Would all their efforts be for nothing? "Thank you." She was so glad he was here to be a support right now. It was the only thing that eased her worry over what might have happened to Sarge. "What's our next step?"

"We search every inch of the ship and keep asking questions. I already retraced where you fell into the rescue boat and searched that whole area and the path that the guy who grabbed Sarge probably took. Did you get a look at the second man?" David started walking and Maya fell in beside him. It felt strange not to be holding on to Sarge's leash seeing his ears bob up and down.

She shook her head. "For a moment. But his face was covered. His hair was sort of blond and was slicked back but obviously bleached because it was black underneath. Kind of distinct."

"I'll tell Noah and Hans to be on the lookout for someone matching that description. He might have been hired help. Since the attacker knew he couldn't keep Sarge out of the way and go after you. All the same, if we could track him down, he might roll on our attacker."

By the time they had searched all the decks as well as the public spots in crew quarters and questioned hundreds of people, it was close to ten o'clock. Neither Hans nor Noah had found any sign of the dog. They'd stopped to get some takeout from one the cafés and headed back to the security office with heavy hearts.

Maya walked holding her take-out container. The aroma of sweet and sour chicken wafted up making her mouth water. They ate while they walked. She knew going so long without food would make it harder to think clearly and therefore conduct the search, but she didn't like slowing down for even a minute.

"While we're at the security office we can check the monitors to see if we can spot Sarge," David said.

"I want to keep looking." She tossed her empty take-out container in a trash can.

"We can cover a lot more ground via the security cameras. We need to switch up our tactics."

He was right. Searching the ship aimlessly could be a time waster when time was precious. "Okay."

They walked to the security office.

David unlocked it and pushed the door open.

"Is there anywhere else we can look to find Sarge, that we haven't already covered?"

David stepped to one side so she could go in first. "We could search the private cabins, but doing something like that involves some paperwork."

They stepped inside. "Maybe we can get the ball rolling on that." She settled in one of the chairs by the security monitors.

"Sure," David said.

Though she knew David would never say it, something in his tone of voice indicated that he thought Sarge was dead.

Maybe it would be a futile effort to keep looking, but she refused to lose hope. They watched the monitors for about five minutes seeing no sign of Sarge.

David swiveled his chair to face her. His voice filled with compassion. "Maya, I have some work-related things I need to take care of here in the office. But I'll still be watching the cameras. Meanwhile, I'm going to get Noah to come back on shift and keep looking for Sarge and asking questions. We will do everything we can to find him. If you want, Noah can come and escort you back to your room as well. You should rest."

"I think I'd rather stay here with you," Maya said.

David's blue eyes studied her. "Okay, there's a cot back in the break room. Why don't you try to get some sleep? You've been through a lot today, physically and emotionally. And judging from how quickly you got in touch with me, I take it you never got around to the doctor checking you out."

"You figured out I escaped from the EMTs?"

"Yes, I kind thought that's what happened."

She glanced in the direction David had indicated the break room was. Shuffling into the little room which consisted of a cot and blanket and file cabinets, she closed the door and clicked off the light. Then lay down, pulling the soft cover up to her chin.

Though her body was fatigued, sleep came slowly as worry about Sarge plagued her thoughts. She did finally feel herself drifting off.

Hours later, she was roused by David's voice as he shook her shoulder. "Maya, wake up. You're not going to believe what I just saw."

As he woke Maya from her slumber, David could not hide his elation. "While I was watching the monitors, guess who ran by on the screen?"

Maya sat upright. "Sarge! You saw my partner?" She'd gone from asleep to fully alert.

David stepped back and clicked on the light. He hadn't wanted to disturb her by turning it on. "Yes, in the stern of the ship where the wave pool is. Let's go."

Maya swung her legs off the cot and slipped

into her shoes which she'd taken off before she fell asleep. "Do you suppose he got away from that guy who grabbed him?" She stood up.

"Maybe. My guess is if he did there were bite marks involved. If anyone comes into the infirmary with that kind of an injury, we have our accomplice. I'll call and send Noah over there to find out."

After making the call to Noah to check the infirmary, they hurried through the security office. David locked the door. The wave pool was three decks up. Both of them broke into a trot as they headed toward the elevator. "You say he ran across the screen?"

"Dragging his leash like he'd escaped," David said.

Maya let out a laugh and shook her head. "That's my buddy."

"I watched the screen to see if he ran back across it and then switched to the areas close to where he was last spotted but couldn't see him anywhere. The only way he could move to a different deck was if he got into the elevator with someone or waited until a stairwell door was open."

"And since there is an all-points bulletin out on him, the second he was spotted someone would phone it in."

Maya was right. Anyone who saw the dog

would know to call security. But at this early a.m. hour most people were sleeping.

Once they were on the deck where the wave pool was, David led her through a corridor that was used by staff and crew but not the public. He needed a card key to open some of the doors, but they would get to the pool that much faster.

They came out to the open area by the wave pool which was turned off at this hour. Surfboards for passengers to use were stored against one wall. The air smelled like chlorine. The pool area had a glass sky dome and lots of plants all around the deck. David walked the perimeter until he found a tropical plant that served as a sort of landmark. "When I saw him on screen this is the way he ran. Past this plant and off in that direction." There were six different entrances that led to the pool that surrounded the seating area around the pool. Four of them did not have doors.

Because the screen had shown only a portion of the pool area, Sarge could have gone down any of the corridors that didn't have doors. The most efficient thing would be to split up and do a search of each of the possible escape routes, but he couldn't risk Maya being attacked again. He needed to stay close to her.

Each of the entries would lead to a different

part of the deck. They had a lot of territory to cover. Sooner or later though the dog would have to come to a closed door and turn around.

"If he's close and can hear me, Sarge will come when I call him."

"Let's be methodical and work our way down each corridor."

Maya pointed toward the hallway closest to them. They hurried down that corridor which led to a book store and snack shop, both of which were closed. The hallway then opened up to a wider shopping corridor which gave them an open view of the area. The retail shops would all be locked up at this hour. Unless her K-9 partner was hiding behind a plant, they would see him.

She called out Sarge's name. Her voice was filled with anguish.

"At least we know he's alive," he said quietly. "We'll find him, Maya. By morning, people will be wandering the ship. He'll be spotted."

"As long as those two men don't get to him first."

"Let's keep looking." His thought was that if Sarge didn't turn up soon, it might be more productive to watch the monitors from the security office. Noah was already on duty, but he could wake Hans and send him out to patrol the deck where Sarge most likely was.

They continued their search through a hall-way that had little boutique shops that opened up into a courtyard which featured some kids' playground equipment and benches for sitting. There was even a hot dog vendor cart, and an ice cream truck which was a golf cart that pulled a trailer behind it. Both carts were shut down and covered with a tarp.

David's radio indicated he had a call. He pulled it from his belt and pressed the talk button. "Go ahead, Noah."

"No one came into the infirmary with a dog bite, but I spotted a guy in one of the casinos that had the hair Maya described. Blond and slicked back. He fessed up right away that he'd been hired to take the dog for money. Appar-ently, he has gambling debt that's through the roof. He let the dog go when he was told to kill it and said he just lied to the other guy that he did the deed. He never saw the man who hired him. The communication was via text, differ-ent number every time."

So, his theory that the second guy was hired help had been confirmed but it was a dead end in every other way. "Thanks for the good po-lice work, Noah."

"No problem."

David turned his attention back to the search. Maya continued to call her dog and checked all the places in the open area Sarge might be. "Maybe he's hurt and can't come to me."

"We'll work the other corridors and then we'll go farther out." He pulled his phone out of his pocket. "I'm going to get Hans out of bed to help us with the search." When the other officers were on duty they could be reached by radio, but during off hours he had to call them.

His phone rang. It wasn't a number he recognized, but it had come in on the emergency line. The ship did not have a dispatcher. David clicked on the talk button.

"Chief Officer Garrison Alaska Dream security," he said.

It was a woman's voice filled with anguish. "My husband and I are here with a young woman who was just attacked."

A tight knot formed at the back of David's neck and his mouth went dry.

"Ma'am, I'm on my way. Where are you?"

"The little enclosed lounge off the upper deck. The young woman is quite upset. She said the man had a knife. If my husband and I hadn't heard her scream, who knows what would have happened."

David sucked in air through his teeth. "Was he wearing a mask?"

The woman didn't answer right away. He

heard mumbling as if she was talking to someone. "She says yes, he was wearing a mask."

"Stay where you are. On my way." David clicked his phone off.

Maya's voice had become flat. "There's been another attack, hasn't there?"

David nodded. "I need to go take her statement. You'll have to come with me."

She grabbed his arm. "No, I want to stay here and keep searching for Sarge. If the man just attacked that woman, he's not on this deck."

"He fled the scene Maya. We don't know where he is."

Her expression was filled with distress.

"He could be on his way here."

"And he might have assumed both Sarge and I are dead and that's why he felt free to attack that woman."

She had a point. While the killer was focused on Maya, the attacks on other women had stopped. "All we know is he is roaming the ship. I just can't take a chance with you wandering around alone—look what happened when we split up for just a few minutes. Please, Maya, we can't delay."

She blew out a breath. "Fine. I'll go. But on the condition that you can get Hans or Noah to come get me and help with the search?"

"Deal. I'll make the call as we head up to the upper deck. It shouldn't take more than fifteen minutes for them to come up and escort you back down here to continue looking for Sarge.

It will be helpful to my investigation if I heard what this victim had to say anyway," Maya said.

"I agree. Let's go."

On their way up in the elevator, David made a call to Hans who didn't pick up. He then tried Noah via the radio. David explained the situation. Noah promised to be on the upper deck as fast as he could get there.

The elevator doors slid open and they stepped out onto a quiet part of the upper deck. The storm had passed and there was a light breeze beneath a starry sky.

Maya stayed one step behind him as he hurried to the lounge where the victim was. He could tell her mind was on finding Sarge, but knew he could count on her professionalism and focus once they began the interview. Traumatic incidents like this attack tended to become less accurate and fuzzier the longer the victim waited to do the interview. He prayed that they would come up with some new evidence that would lead them to the man with the knife.

He opened the door to the lounge where a

young woman with long brown hair was being held by another woman who looked to be in her forties while a man who was probably her husband sat close by.

The woman with the long hair looked up when David and Maya walked in.

"I'm head security officer David Garrison. Can you tell me your name?"

"Hannah Stevenson." The woman glanced at Maya as if seeking an explanation for who she was.

Maya stepped forward. "I'm helping officer Garrison with this investigation."

The vague explanation seemed to satisfy Hannah.

David pulled out a notebook. He took a chair opposite the young woman. "If I could just ask you a few questions…" He noted the fresh scratches on Hannah's bare shoulder. "And then we will take you down to the ship's medical facility to have you checked out."

Hannah was dressed in an off-the-shoulder gown that sparkled.

"Were you just ballroom dancing?" Maya asked gently.

Hannah brightened at the question. "Yes. It was crew night to have the ballroom. I work at the information desk."

The attacker, who they knew was a member

of the crew, had probably been at the ballroom as well, scouting for his next victim. Since he may have assumed that both Maya and Sarge were dead, he felt free to continue going after women.

"I know this has probably been very frightening for you," Maya said.

"Yes," Hannah drew her attention to the older woman who still had her arm wrapped around her back. "If these two hadn't come along when they did… I don't know what would have happened."

"Is there anything you remember about your attacker? I know you couldn't see his face."

"He was in a tux. Unless he was a waiter in one of the higher-end restaurants, he must have been at the ballroom as well." Hannah rubbed her bare arms.

The man who had been sitting close took off his jacket and draped it over the younger woman's shoulders. "This is a terrible thing to happen. Hannah is our daughter's age."

"Is there anything at all you remember?" David asked. "Did the man say anything to you?"

"Yes, he said, 'All you beautiful women are alike.'" Hannah shuddered and the older woman drew her close.

That sounded like a man who had been hurt by a woman.

Noah popped his head in. "I'm here to give Maya a hand."

"We're just finishing up," said David. He hoped the comment would communicate to Maya that is was okay for her to go. "Unless you have any more questions Maya?"

Maya rose to her feet. "I'll catch up with you later Officer Garrison. We'll talk."

David did not fail to catch the tinge of emotion in her voice. She was torn between doing her job and finding her partner. He knew Maya was keeping things formal in front of the witness and the passengers. Still, he wished he could have offered his support for finding Sarge by giving her a hug.

As he turned his attention back to Hannah, a debate was raging in his head. She had been able to get away, but maybe the next woman wouldn't. So far, the attacks and even the murder had been kept mostly under the radar. David knew for the safety of the female passengers that the time had come to issue a public warning about being alone on any of the decks, and maybe even close off this upper deck since the killer seemed to that location. But he also knew that when he called the cruise line owner he would meet with resistance. Once the announcement about taking precautions was made, some people might want to disembark and get their money back when they got into port.

He escorted Hannah down to the infirmary. The older couple stayed with her.

David headed out of the infirmary with a heavy heart. He had some important decisions to make before morning, but first he knew he needed to get some sleep, at least a couple of hours.

He texted Noah to let him know he was returning to his cabin but would be up in a couple of hours. Then he asked about Sarge.

The reply text came just as David opened the door to his cabin.

No sign of the dog. We will continue the search. Maya refuses to give up.

It felt like a knife had gone into his chest. More than anything he wanted to be with her to help and to console. But going without sleep for so long meant he would be no good to anyone.

All the same, there was no place in the world he would rather be than with Maya. He hated seeing her so torn up.

As he fell asleep, he prayed that Sarge was okay.

THIRTEEN

Maya sat in front of the monitors feeling her eyelids grow heavy. When she and Noah finally had to call the search for Sarge off, Noah had agreed to let her into the security office so she could watch the screens for any sign of her dog. She promised to call him if she saw any sign of Sarge. As long as David was getting some much-needed sleep, Noah would be there to guard her and help in finding Sarge.

She watched the screens and clicked through the various areas on the deck where the wave pool was. Then she searched all the other areas on the ship that had security cameras. The only thing she saw was Noah walking a patrol on an empty deck.

Sarge just had to be *somewhere* on this ship. What scared her though was that maybe he had been taken again. It just seemed like a dog on the run would be spotted sooner or later even with most of the passengers asleep.

As her eyes closed, her head snapped back and then forward. Resting her cheek on her hand she laid her head on the counter by the keyboard. Maybe if she took a power nap, she'd get her energy back.

The next thing she was aware of was the smell of fresh coffee. She raised her head. David was standing beside her and had placed a steaming mug on the counter by her.

He smiled.

She laughed. "You seem really perky."

"I only needed a couple hours sleep to get my mojo back. Looks like you got a little shut-eye too."

Maya self-consciously wiped her mouth, wondering if she'd been drooling in her sleep. She glanced at the clock on the wall. It was four in the morning. She'd been asleep for an hour. "Not on purpose."

She stared at the screen. Still no activity. She knew that as soon as the hour was reasonable, she was going to have to call Lorenza and let her know Sarge was missing. The thought made her feel even more hopeless.

David took a sip of his coffee. "In another hour the morning kitchen crews will be in full force getting ready for the breakfast crowd. Then you'll see the shop owners opening up. There is a rhythm to life on the Alaska Dream."

"That sounds kind of neat. It's like a floating village…and you are the village constable."

David laughed and sat down beside her. He ran his hands through his hair and let out a heavy breath. "As soon as the hour is decent, I'm going to need to call the owner and have a serious talk. He wanted all of this to be under the radar as much as possible. But given that last attack on Hannah, I think we will have to put out a general warning for women to not be alone on decks or anywhere they might be vulnerable." A muscle ticked in his jaw. "It may cost me my job, but the safety of the passengers has to be my top priority."

"I couldn't agree more." As she stared into David's blue eyes, she felt a deep admiration for him. "But a tough choicc all the same."

David nodded. He pointed to the dorm-size fridge with the microwave on top of it. "I think we have some precooked sausage and egg sandwiches I can heat up if you're hungry."

"Sure, that sounds good." While he pulled food out of the little freezer and put it the microwave, she drew her attention back to the security screens. Maya took a sip of her coffee, enjoying the warmth and taste, then leaned forward to study each picture more intently.

A man in a chef uniform walked across one of the screens. "What if Sarge has been taken to crew living quarters. Is there any way we could see that, at least the hallways, dining hall and laundry?"

"There are no security cameras in the crew area. We can search it on foot." He set a sausage sandwich on a paper plate in front of her. "First breakfast."

"Okay good, that's what we will do."

David turned his chair, so it faced her. "You know, Maya, I want to find Sarge as badly as you do, but at some point, we might have to accept that he's not on the ship anymore."

Though his comment was spoken with great tenderness, it still felt like a knife through her heart. She did not want to face that possibility. "I think it's too early to give up. If he's running free, he would have shown up somewhere or been spotted. I think the attacker saw him and grabbed him." She touched her hand to her heart. "I feel it in here. He's still alive."

He nodded. "Okay, we'll keep looking. If I get security calls, I'll have to deal with them."

"I get that," Maya said as the heaviness of despair filled her. "I just think that someone would have to have a really black heart to kill a dog or throw it overboard. The accomplice couldn't bring himself to do it."

"We are dealing with a man who has killed a woman."

The tightness through Maya's chest was so intense that she laid her palm on her heart. Nothing David was saying was untrue—she was just having a hard time accepting it.

They finished their breakfast and coffee. No security calls had yet come in. "Let's go search the crew area." She stood up and gave a final glance at the screen. Movement caught her eye. Sarge dragging his leash raced across the screen. "Did you see that?" She pointed to the screen where she'd seen her dog. "He was there! Where is that?"

David looked at the screen. "That's the corridor by the botanical gardens and the kids' activity room. But it's not on the same deck as the wave pool. Wonder how he got up there."

Feeling a joy she almost couldn't contain, Maya moved toward the door. "Let's go get him."

They raced through the ship, passing early rising passengers and crew members getting ready for a day of work. Once they got to the botanical gardens Maya called out Sarge's name. She heard barking but could not see him anywhere. They were in a jungle.

Both of them moved toward the sound of Sarge's barking.

"Why isn't he coming to me?" She couldn't contain her excitement.

The botanical gardens were beneath a dome. The room was kept warm to aid the growth of the tropical plants. The air was thick and humid. Maya pushed past the plants, running ahead of David.

Sarge's barking got louder as she hurried around a display of orchids. The K-9 was there tied to an iron bench. Something clicked in her brain. When they'd seen Sarge on the screen he'd been running free. He could not have gotten to the deck alone. "This is a trap." Sarge had been used as bait to lure her there. She turned to warn David, but all she saw was his arm on the floor sticking out from a bush. Her brain barely registered that he'd been knocked out when the masked man jumped out from behind a lattice wall of flowers.

Maya screamed. Sarge barked and jerked on his leash. The assailant came at her with the knife. She dodged out of the way, then reached her leg out to try and hit him behind the knees so he would fall to the ground. He avoided her and raised the knife above his head. As the knife came toward her shoulder, she blocked the move by grabbing the man's wrist and then landing a blow to his stomach with her other hand. She pressed on the nerves of his hand to try to get him to drop the knife.

As they struggled, she was only inches from the masked man's face. His eyes held a wild dancing quality. "You're going to die."

She reached up with her free hand to grab his mask.

He stepped back to prevent her from seeing who he was. The distraction gave her time to bang the hand that held the knife against the wall. He dropped the knife and grabbed his wrist.

A moaning sound came from where David had been disabled.

The attacker tilted his head and then took off running still holding his hand, probably frightened at the prospect of having to fight two people. Maya hurried to free Sarge, taking note of where the attacker had gone. David, who still seemed wobbly on his feet, came and stood beside her. "You okay?"

David nodded.

"Sarge can track that knife," said Maya. "The trail is still hot."

"Let's go."

With Sarge taking the lead, they sprinted through corridors and down a deck. The direction they were going felt vaguely familiar. Then she remembered, that first night when she'd been attacked this was where Sarge had taken her. They ended up outside the same main kitchen on deck three.

Sarge alerted.

David opened the door. The place was busy with crew preparing breakfast. Grills sizzled and the smell of bacon was heavy in the air.

The dog whined. David let go of the swinging door and peered down at the trash can outside the kitchen.

He pointed. "I'm going to need an evidence bag."

Maya peered into the garbage can where the knife had been tossed.

"I can probably find something in the kitchen to use as an evidence bag. Let's go in and see if we can find a man with green eyes."

Maya had a feeling that the perp had probably passed through the kitchen out a back entrance or the service elevator just like the first time. They entered the kitchen where David retrieved a plastic bag to store the knife along with some disposable gloves used to handle the food. While he questioned the busy kitchen staff, Maya wandered around the counters making eye contact with every man of medium build. The attacker had been dressed in black pants and a gray shirt. No one here was dressed like that. Though it would have been easy enough to don a white chef's smock. None of the men avoided her gaze. None of them appeared to have green eyes.

David came over to her. "From talking to the folks in here, there is a ton of crew traffic this time of day. No one going through was a strange face. You know what that means?"

Her mood lifted. "Our suspect works out of this kitchen. That narrows down the possibilities substantially." They were getting closer to catching this guy.

"I'll grab that knife, and we can go look at employee records."

After retrieving the knife from the garbage and placing it in the bag, they hurried back to the security office to look through employee records. They stopped to grab some food for Sarge. Once in the security office, David found some containers for the food and water. Sarge ate heartily. Maya sat down on the floor beside him and rubbed his ears. There hadn't been time to show how happy she was that he was safe and sound until now. "I don't think he's been fed since they took him. Poor guy."

Sarge stopped eating long enough to lean into her touch as she petted his back and front shoulder. "So glad to have you back on duty, buddy."

The dog wagged his tail.

Maya drew her attention back up to where David was tapping the keyboard and scrutinizing the computer screen. "This shouldn't take long. We are looking at thirty guys who work out of the kitchen. We can eliminate anyone who is not of average build. I'm going to print out all the employee IDs, which will list their eye color." He pushed several buttons.

She heard a printer running but wasn't sure where it was kept. David opened a cabinet underneath the counter and pulled out a stack of papers. He divided them and handed her a stack.

The IDs were printed out in black-and-white but referenced eye color. Maya sorted through her stack coming up with two men whose eye color was listed as green. She studied each picture ID feeling a chill run down her spine. "I got two."

"I got two possibilities as well." He reached over for her stack. "So now we text each of these four men saying we want to question them. I won't say why, just that the security office wants to talk to them."

"Do you have an interview room?"

"No, but there's a small conference room in one of the administrative rooms that will suffice. Let me send out the texts."

Maya knew that a smart criminal would

show up for the interview and tell lies. She'd had some training in watching body language to figure out if a man was being honest in his answers. "I'd like to help with the interviews."

Again, David offered her his forty-watt smile. "Of course, that goes without saying. Your help has been invaluable."

He sent off the texts. All four men responded, and a time was set up to interview each one of them. Maya, Sarge and David left the office on several calls, including a case of a teenage boy stealing from a shop and that of an older man who had lost his wallet. As they worked together, Maya was struck by how compassionate David was in dealing with the teenager and the senior citizen.

Once Hans was on duty to take the calls that came in, they hurried to the interview room. The first two men came in. David asked each man the same set of questions about their whereabouts at the times the attacks had taken place along with some other inquiries that might expose their guilt.

For the most part, Maya remained silent and simply studied the reactions of the men. From the moment they came into the room, she watched their expressions when they saw her. None of them showed any sign of recognition. She did see a little fear in one of the men's eyes when his gaze landed on Sarge as he sat at attention beside her, a very normal reaction. Despite his size, Sarge could be intimidating when he wanted to be. He seemed to understand that that was his role for these interviews.

The second suspect left, and they waited for the third man. The interviews were set up to last twenty minutes. Five minutes went by.

"Who is it we are waiting for?"

David sifted through the stack of papers and pushed one across the table. Maya stared down at the black-and-white copy of the photo ID, Joel Morris. They waited for Joel. Five minutes passed then five more.

"Our number three suspect is not going to show," said Maya.

"No, he's not." David tapped his fingers on the table. "And unless he has a real good reason for not showing, it kind of makes him look guilty."

Then the fourth suspect came in for questioning. David interviewed the man for only five minutes and then told him he was free to go. That crew member clearly was not culpable.

They were both thinking the same thing. Joel Morris was the man they were after.

FOURTEEN

Though it seemed like a futile activity, David, Maya and Sarge all hurried down to the crew living quarters to Joel Morris's cabin. If Joel knew they were on to him, he was probably hiding out somewhere on the ship. Maybe it would have been smarter to track down each of the men and question them. Hard to say.

They came to the door of Joel's cabin. David glanced in Maya's direction. "You and Sarge be on high alert? We know what kind of violence he's capable of. Just in case he is in his cabin…"

"We're ready for anything," Maya said.

He knocked on the cabin door. "Joel Morris, this is David Garrison, head of ship security. We need to talk to you."

A groggy male voice came from behind the door. "Joel isn't here."

Must be Joel's cabinmate. "Sir, can you please open the door? We need to talk to you."

David heard some shuffling and banging and an expletive. All the cabins had only one exit. The man wasn't going anywhere.

The door swung open and a disheveled man with uncombed hair stood on the threshold. He blinked over and over again.

"Sorry we woke you up, but we need to ask you some questions about Joel Morris. Is he your roommate?"

"Yes."

Maya stepped forward. "And can you tell us your name?"

The man lifted his head and blinked several times. "I'm Wayne Hawkins."

"When was the last time you saw Joel?" David asked.

"The reason why we make such good roommates is because we work opposite shifts. He starts in the early morning and I work the concert venues at night as a bartender." Wayne ran his hands through his messy hair. "We haven't run into each other for like a day."

Maya stepped sideways so she was visible to the man. "How long have you been his roommate?"

"Eight months."

"Have you noticed any changes in the last week or so," she asked.

Wayne tilted his head to the side. "Right

before we left Seattle, he was pretty torn up about his girlfriend finding someone else and then quitting the ship."

"How torn up?" she murmured.

"He threw things around the room, put a fist through the wall and called her every name in the book." He shrugged. "I guess I should have reported it."

"Can I ask what the girlfriend looked like?" Maya spoke up.

"She was way out of Joel's league. Super-model material."

"Did she have long brown hair?" David asked.

"Yes," he answered.

Now they had a motive for the attacks and the murder. Joel was going after women who reminded him of the one who had betrayed him.

"We're so sorry to have bothered you. I know about late night shifts," David said. "Hope you are able to go back to sleep. If you see Joel or hear about where he is, you need to get in touch with me right away."

"Wow, that sounds serious. What's going on?"

"We need to question him about some incidents that have taken place on the ship," Maya explained.

The roommate's eyes grew a little wider. "Yeah, I saw that bulletin about women needing to be careful about being alone. Seriously, Joel might be the guy who's going after women?"

"We can't say anything at this point," David said. "It's just very important that he get in touch with us. If he does return to the room or you see him, please let us know."

Wayne tugged on the collar of his baggy worn T-shirt. "For sure. I'll do that."

"Thanks again," Maya said.

The roommate moved to close the door.

"Hang on." David caught the door. "Does he have any favorite places he likes to go on the ship. Entertainment venues? Sports things?"

"Honestly, we don't talk that much. The one thing I do know is that him and his lady love used to meet on that upper deck at night cause it usually is not very crowded."

Now the attacks on the upper deck made even more sense.

"Sure. I'll let you know right away if he comes around." Wayne said. "Anything else?"

Maya spoke up. "Is there something of Joel's that we might borrow that would have his scent on it. A T-shirt he wore recently or something like that?"

Maya was one step ahead of him, David

thought admiringly. The next thing to do in locating Joel was combing the whole ship to find him. Using Sarge to sniff him out would make that search much easier.

The roommate turned sideways staring at the clutter in the cabin. "Give me a second… I'll find something." He stepped away from the door. They could hear him rummaging around.

The guy returned with a shirt which he handed to Maya.

David piped up. "Can we ask that you not touch, put away or dispose of any of Joel's belongings?"

"Sure not a problem."

"One more thing. Is there anyone else who Joel was close to who might be able to shed some light on where he might be on the ship?"

Wayne shrugged. "He kind of kept to himself. Maybe someone in the kitchen he worked out of would know. To be honest with you, I always thought he was a little out there and then after his breakup, he kind of scared me. I don't blame the lady for breaking up with him."

"We'll be back in touch."

The roommate closed the door.

"I'm going to get all of the ship's security team on duty for the search. If we can't track Joel down, the next step is to put out a bulletin to the public. Something that says, 'Have you seen this man? He's wanted for questioning in some crimes on the ship.' We have to be careful not to imply any guilt or the case could be thrown out once it goes to court."

Maya held the T-shirt they'd been given. "Sarge is trained to track weapons, but a dog's nose is a hundred times better than anything we could do."

"Let me make the calls to Hans and Noah and then we'll get started."

"That sounds good," said Maya. "I need to call my boss and let her know that we have a suspect and are searching for him. Once we have in in custody, the K-9 Unit will make arrangements to transport him when we get into port."

Both of them made their respective phone calls. Within minutes, they were ready to begin a shipwide search.

As promised, David got the rest of the security team on board with what needed to happen. Hans would help with the search and Noah would go down to the kitchen that Joel had worked out of to question his coworkers to find any leads on where he might be hiding. Maya placed the T-shirt by Sarge's nose. The dog stood at attention and licked his chops.

Maya gave the command and they were off

and running. The search took them through the ship but dead-ended by the wave pool.

"The scent of the chlorine might be messing with Sarge's ability to track," she said. "Let's pull him out of this area and see if we can get him back on track. He needs to find a fresh scent."

Maya steered her partner into a corridor and then placed the T-shirt under the dog's nose again. Sarge whimpered.

"He's confused," Maya said. "I'm not sure what's happening." She rubbed the Malinois's ears. "I wonder if the scent is bringing back how he was treated by Joel. Being abducted is just as traumatic for a dog as it is for a person." Maya put her face close to Sarge's and rubbed his ears.

"Poor guy," David said.

She looked up at him. "What if we just keep walking and searching? Maybe he'll pick up on something."

After several hours, both David and Maya admitted to feeling discouraged. They stopped to grab hot dogs to eat and got a container of water for Sarge.

David's radio made a static noise. He pressed the talk button. "What is it?"

Noah's voice came across the line. "Been asking a lot of questions of Joel's coworkers.

Not coming up with much, but several of them did mention that he liked to go to movies when he wasn't working."

"Okay, we'll head over to the movie theater. Thanks, Noah."

"All the kitchen crew knows we're looking for him. They are the ones most likely to recognize him anyway," Noah added.

"I agree. Putting something out to the public might cause unnecessary fear. Stay in touch." David clicked off his radio and looked at Maya. "We're headed to the theater."

"I have no idea where the theater is."

Maya's heartbeat clicked up a notch when David said they were going to search the theater. Maybe they were getting closer. There were a thousand places someone could hide on this ship. If Joel didn't return to his cabin though, where would he sleep? On a deck chair?

So far, from what Noah had indicated Joel didn't have friends who might let him hide in their cabin. That meant he probably had to stay in the public places. Though, a crew member might know of some tucked-away places no one would think to search.

They hurried past a corridor of shops and turned down a side corridor where the signs indicated the direction of the theater. There was even a marquee out front that advertised two movie choices: a classic Western and a kids' movie. When they checked the movie times, it looked like the Western had started twenty minutes ago.

They entered the back of the dark theater. Sarge heeled beside Maya. The movie flickered on the screen. Though it was hard to see, it looked like the theater was maybe half-full. If Joel Morris was in here, how were they going to find him and keep him from fleeing? Maybe they could wait until the film was over and watch the people come out. The movie had started only twenty minutes ago though, and there were two exits at the front of the theater by the screen through which someone could escape unnoticed if they wanted to.

David pointed, indicating that she and Sarge would take one aisle and he would take the other. "No flashlights," he whispered. "We don't want to give him a chance to get away."

Maya wasn't sure if not using flashlights would make a difference. Even in the dark, David's uniform was easy to spot and Sarge as well would cause a panic to Joel Morris if he barked. As she worked her way down the aisle, row by row, no one seemed alarmed. Though some people glanced in her direction most kept their attention on the film.

A gunfight scene erupted on the screen which made it impossible to hear anything else. When she was nearly to the first row, Sarge tugged on his leash indicating the back of the theater by the main exit they had come through. Though her eyes were still not completely adjusted to the lack of light, she thought she saw a figure—she could not tell if it was a man or woman—get up and slip out.

She hurried back up the aisle. A woman holding the hand of a small child had gotten up and blocked her way.

The woman whispered, "Do you know where the bathroom is?"

"Nice doggie," the little boy said.

"I don't know where the bathroom is. Scuse me," Maya moved to arc around the woman and child so she could reach the exit where the person had gone. She stepped out into the bright lights. Plenty of people were walking around the shops and places to eat. She scanned back and forth. None of the men seemed in a hurry and no one looked like Joel.

A man walking casually with a hat pulled down low over his face caught her attention. She and Sarge ran toward the man but when he looked in her direction, she saw that it wasn't Joel.

Maya led Sarge back into the theater. She didn't see David anywhere.

The man sitting at the end of the row she was standing by tugged on her sleeve. "He went that way in a hurry."

The man pointed to one of the two exits at the front of the theater. With Sarge heeling beside her, Maya hurried toward the exit. David must have seen something. She pulled the curtain aside that blocked the exit and stepped into what appeared to be a dark hallway.

Sarge pulled on the leash and yipped. The level of excitement he exhibited suggested that his powerful K-9 nose had picked up on something.

"Wait." Maya fumbled for her phone to turn on the flashlight app.

Sarge got even more excited. She shone the light all around. They were in a wide hallway that looked like it was used for storage. There were lots of boxes, totes and movie posters. Now that she had some light, she could see the door at the other end of it that led back outside.

Sarge yanked on the leash. At first, she thought he was headed toward the door, but then he lunged at a stack of totes. The totes started to wobble.

A man jumped out at her from behind them and lunged at her. She dropped her phone as she twisted to get away. Sarge barked. The dog had grabbed hold of the man's pant leg and was tugging.

Though she could not see, it was clear this had to be Joel. Maya struggled to get away when the man grabbed her arm and twisted it behind her back. He pushed her arm up so far it hurt. He leaned close enough that she felt his hot breath on the back of her neck. "I've had about enough of you."

A door slammed somewhere. The attacker pushed her hard from behind. The impact of hitting the floor knocked the wind out of her. Was she hearing David's voice or just imagining it?

David returned through the theater exit door when he realized after a quick search that Joel had not gone out the door but had probably hidden behind the boxes. When he shone his light, he saw Maya falling to the floor and Joel kicking Sarge to get away from him. The dog yipped in pain.

The perp took off back toward the theater. Someone must have heard the ruckus because the lights were on and people had gotten out of their seats. The movie continued to flicker on the screen. Joel got around the people by jumping over seats.

"Stop, security!" David yelled.

Joel pushed the people attempting to stop him out out of the way and disappeared into the main corridor. David hurried up the aisle as folks stepped aside so he could get to the main exit.

Heart pounding, David stepped out into the busy thoroughfare. A lot of passengers were strolling around. He could see quite far up and down the corridor. Of course, Joel would stop running and blend in. There had been nothing distinct in what Joel had been wearing. All neutral colors meant that he would blend into background pretty easily. David studied the shoppers and clusters of people for at least a minute before giving up hope of finding Joel. He radioed the other two officers letting them know the last place Joel had been spotted. David spoke into his radio. "He had on a beige shirt and gray pants. He was wearing a black baseball hat but it fell off in the fight he had with Maya and Sarge. Medium height, medium build, brown hair."

Noah came on the line. "He might try to grab another hat somewhere to hide his face, right?"

"Maybe. If you could keep searching, I'll send Hans into the security room to see if he can spot anything on the cameras in this area.

I'll be back to help as soon as I make sure Maya isn't hurt."

After signing off, David turned and raced back into the theater toward the exit by the screen. He could hear Sarge barking even before he pulled back the curtain to see if Maya was okay.

One of the moviegoers standing close to the exit curtain said, "We tried to get in there to help that woman, but that dog won't let anyone close."

When Sarge saw David, he stopped barking and wagged his tail. David dove down to the floor and gathered Maya in his arms. Sarge licked David's face and whined.

She opened her mouth, but no words came out. Was she in pain. Had she broken something?

He drew her closer. David addressed the three people who had pulled back the curtain and were peering in. "Can someone call for a medic?"

"Sure," said an older man.

"I'm okay." Her voice was shaky.

"Hey." Joy surged through him when she looked at him. "You're back."

"Did you get Joel?"

David shook his head. "Hans and Noah are still searching."

"I'm sure they need our help." Maya tried to sit up but fell back down into his arms. She was weak from the fight she'd been in.

"First, we need to get you checked out and make sure it's nothing serious."

"That is precious time that we'll lose."

"True. But I don't want you passing out because you have some sort of serious injury going on. If you need to rest a few hours, so be it. Sarge and I will continue the search."

She smiled. "Yes, Sarge seems to have taken a liking to you." She reached out to pet the dog. Sarge responded by licking her cheek.

The EMTs popped their heads in, a man and woman who looked like they could have been twins, both blond and slender. David knew the woman's name was Vicky, but her male partner must be a new hire. "We got a stretcher for her."

"She was pushed hard," David said, looking back toward her.

"Did you hit your head or anything?" Vicky dove in with a tiny penlight which she shone on Maya's eyes. "Pupils aren't dilated."

"Is it even worth it to take me back to the infirmary?" Maya touched her arm and winced.

Vicky sat back on her toes. "It's always good to have the doc check you out. What's going on with your arm?"

"He twisted it really severely and then when I fell forward it took most of the impact."

"Might be fractured." The male EMT stepped closer. "Why don't we get her on the stretcher?"

The medics both rose to their feet and pushed the stretcher into the storage/hallway area.

As Vicky and her partner lifted Maya, she grasped David's sleeve. "Take care of Sarge for me."

"Will do. I'm sure he will be a help. I'll check with you in a bit or you can text me when you are given the okay to be released. Don't leave the infirmary alone."

As she was laid on the stretcher, she lifted a hand to indicate she agreed. He assumed that with medical personal around the infirmary and all of the crew on the lookout for Joel that Maya would be okay. He prayed he wasn't wrong.

FIFTEEN

Maya heard her phone beep that she had a text while the doctor, a woman with a grand-motherly disposition, checked her out. It was clear that the shipboard medical facilities had limited equipment. After doing an X-ray which showed no break, most of the doctor's examination involved asking a host of questions and turning Maya's arm and inquiring if it hurt.

Maya wondered if the text was from David. Maybe they had tracked down Joel.

The doctor held a penlight vertical in her hand. "Maya, I'm going to move this light across your field of vision. Please follow it with your gaze."

Maya complied with the doctor's wishes. "I didn't hit my head."

"I don't want to take any chances," the doctor said.

Maya shuddered at the memory of the attack as pain shot through her arm again.

"I think we are looking at a sprain for the arm. Ice it and try to limit use that would cause further damage." The doctor stepped over to a computer that was in the room and typed on a keyboard.

"Okay. Can I go now?"

"Your body and mind have been through a lot with this altercation. Why don't you rest for a little bit and then I will feel comfortable releasing you?"

Maya nodded. Once the doctor left the room, she reached for her phone which was on the rolling table by her bed. The text was not from David as she had hoped. It was from Poppy Walsh, another K-9 officer that Maya worked with.

Have an update on Katie's case with her aunt's reindeer ranch. Call me when you can.

Since the text had come in only a few minutes ago, she could probably catch Poppy. Maya pressed in the number. When she had gotten the temporary phone from the security office, she'd given the new number to Lorenza to forward to the rest of the team.

Poppy picked up right away. "Maya, good to see your name and number pop up on my phone."

The other woman's chipper voice reminded Maya that she longed to be back on shore with the rest of the team. "You did just text me a few minutes ago."

"So I did. Lorenza has made it super clear in the briefings that we need to make sure you are updated on our cases. She wants to ensure you hit the ground running when you get back on dry land. You are coming back, right? You haven't fallen in love with a handsome sailor or something?"

Maya's mind immediately went to David. "No, no handsome sailors on board."

"It's like I hear a smile in your voice. You *have* met someone?"

"Someone I like a great deal, but it's an impossible situation. I assure you as soon as this investigation is wrapped up, I will come ashore and be ready to dive back into my regular work."

"Good to hear," Poppy said. "Anyway, just wanted to let you know what is going on with that reindeer farm that Katie's aunt owns."

Katie was Lorenza's assistant. "Did the surveillance equipment you guys put up show something?" The ranch had suffered harassment, and reindeer had been let out of their pen. All but one was eventually found and then another reindeer was stolen.

"Yes indeed," Poppy said. "We caught a man in black with a hoodie covering his face running around the storage area and the bunkhouse on the ranch. Or should I say sneaking around, because his body language and the time of day all suggest he was up to some kind of mischief. Lorenza thinks if we can catch this guy, we'll get to the bottom of what is going on."

"Obviously from the way the guy was dressed, he didn't want to be identified. Any idea who it might be?"

"Not sure. All the people Katie and her aunt suggested might have something against the ranch had alibis that put them elsewhere."

"What's the team's next move then?"

"Lorenza is posting some private security guards by the place," Poppy said. "We think given the history of theft and destruction of property the guy in the hoodie will come back."

"Let's hope so. At least that's progress, huh?"

"Yes. How are things on board the ship?"

"Well, as I'm sure Lorenza has kept you up to speed. We have a suspect, but he's hiding out somewhere on the ship. He's a crew member so he knows all the good hiding places, and this is a big ship." As she spoke to Poppy, an idea occurred to Maya. Joel did know the ship really well. So wouldn't he go someplace the security cameras weren't likely to spot him, especially after he'd been tracked down in the theater? It seemed like he'd go deeper into the less public parts of the ship.

"Sound like you're getting close to bringing him in," Poppy said.

"We're concerned that once we dock tomorrow morning, he'll slip out into the general population. That doesn't give us much time. I would hate to have identified him as a very prominent suspect only to lose him out in the wide world." Maya felt some of the tension ease from her body. Talking with Poppy about the case, hearing her team member's encouragement, renewed her strength. She and David and the rest of the security team were going to catch this guy.

"I know you Maya, once you narrow in on a suspect you are like a dog on a scent. I bet before too long you'll be telling us that your suspect is in handcuffs and ready to be brought ashore."

"Thanks, Poppy. I needed that pep talk."

"That's what I'm here for."

Maya heard a male voice in the background like someone had come into the room where Poppy was. Her teammate's voice got fainter and Maya could no longer discern what she was saying. She figured she must be talking to the man who had entered the room.

Poppy came back on the line. "I got to go. Lex is here with Danny. We're going to make a picnic lunch and head to the park so Danny can play."

Lex was a park ranger that Poppy had recently worked with on a poaching case in Glacier Bay National Park. They had been romantically involved ten years ago, but it had ended and Lex had married someone else. Lex had lost his wife and been left to raise his son Danny alone until he was reunited with Poppy and they'd rekindled their romance.

Poppy was a year older than Maya. The fact that her colleague had found true love gave Maya some hope that she shouldn't assume that at thirty she was facing a life of singleness.

Maya said her goodbyes to Poppy and hung up.

The nurse popped her head around the curtain. "I heard voices in here. The doctor's orders are that you rest then we'll check you out in a bit."

Still gripping the phone, Maya nodded. "Okay."

The nurse's head disappeared, and Maya waited until the footsteps had receded before she put in a call to David to share her theory about where Joel might be hiding. He didn't pick up, so she texted him. She stared at the phone, half expecting an instantaneous response.

Though her mind was spinning with what to do about catching Joel, she leaned back and shut her eyes. It surprised her how easily sleep overtook her. She woke up in the dark. The nurse must have come in and shut the lights off. When she checked her phone, which had slipped out of her hand when she nodded off, she saw that only a half hour had passed. David still had not responded to her text.

An empty feeling invaded her awareness. She had to admit that getting a text from him lifted her spirits even if it was just about the case.

She could hear whispers and footsteps growing closer. She was reminded of the last time she was in this infirmary and she had wondered if the man they now knew as Joel Morris had come in to do her harm but been scared away. The footsteps grew louder and then took what sounded like an abrupt turn. More hushed voices landed on her ear.

Her phone pinged. She looked at her screen expecting to see David's text response. Instead, the message was from an unknown number, though it was crystal clear to Maya who had sent it.

I'm coming for you Maya. I know who you really are. You are in my way.

Again, she heard approaching footsteps pounding intensely as they came toward her. This time they did not veer off.

Fighting off a sense of defeat, David sat down on a bench to check his texts and email messages. Maybe Hans had spotted something on the security monitors or maybe a call had come in from a passenger who'd seen Joel. Sarge sat at David's feet and gazed up at him. He had to admit the dog had found a way into his heart. He reached out and stroked the K-9's ears and muzzle.

The only text and missed call was from Maya. She hadn't left anything on voicemail, but he was happy that she'd sent a text.

I'm thinking that Joel knows this ship really well. He's going to go somewhere the security cameras can't see him.

True. But where to start? There were parts of the ship that even some of the crew didn't have access to. The engine room for instance. Only the captain and authorized maintenance people could go in there. Joel might steal a card key to get in there to hide. But that seemed like a lot of work and too much risk of being caught. The laundry facilities and other public parts of crew quarters did not have cameras. So that was a possibility. Hans so far hadn't spotted anyone who looked like Joel on the security cameras though it would be nothing to find a hat to cover his face from view.

Maybe he could brainstorm with Maya and come up with a plan. He dialed her number, but it went to voicemail. Maybe she'd turned it off and was sleeping.

He called the desk at the infirmary.

Someone picked up right away. "Alaska Dream infirmary. How may I help you?" A woman's voice came across the line.

"Can you check on Maya Rodriguez for me? She's not answering her phone."

"One second. Stay on the line. It's a short walk."

David heard footsteps and then the nurse spoke up. "She's not in her bed."

David swallowed hard to push down the rising panic. "Do you think she might have left?"

"Maybe, but the doctor requested to check her out one more time before that."

David stood up from the bench. "Maybe she just went to the bathroom or something. I'm on my way there. See you in five."

Sarge whimpered.

"Let's go, buddy. I'm afraid something might have happened to Maya. We sure wouldn't want that, would we? Since we both care about her."

He trotted along toward the infirmary when his phone pinged again. He breathed a sigh of relief. The text was from Maya.

Meet me in the hallway outside the back of the infirmary.

It was easy enough to reroute and head to where Maya had said she was waiting. He and Sarge stepped into a hallway that had three doors connected to it. All of which, judging by the signs on them, held medical supplies. He slipped past the first door and called Maya's name. Maybe she was in the adjoining hallway. Her descriptions of places on the ship could be a little wonky because she didn't use the same lingo that the crew did to describe locations.

Sarge sat on his back haunches and growled. The dog started to turn back in the direction they'd just come.

David had only a moment to register that the door they had just passed was slightly ajar before a jolt of electricity hit his back and he crumpled to the ground. The last sound he heard was Sarge yelping as though in pain.

After realizing that Joel might be coming for her while she was in her hospital bed, Maya had slipped out and hidden in the first place she could find, a closet on the other side of the curtain from where her bed was. It wasn't until she was hiding that she realized in her haste that she had left her phone behind.

Not wanting to draw attention to herself, she waited in silence. When she didn't hear any more footsteps, she returned to her bed. Her phone had been stolen. She hurried to the front desk.

"Did you see anyone come or go through here? A man with brown hair—he may have had a hat on— average build?"

The nurse shook her head. "No, sorry. But the security officer should be here by now. He was on his way to talk to you when you didn't answer your phone."

Maya's heartbeat skipped up a notch. "Is the front entrance the only way in and out of the infirmary?"

"No, there is a back way where we keep our supplies. I'll show you."

The nurse led her past the curtains that served to divide the three hospital beds to a door which she opened. "It goes around the corner and then into a hallway."

"Thank you."

Maya hurried around the corner. She gasped at what she saw. Sarge lying prone, his legs jerking spastically. David flat on his face, not moving. And a man kneeling over Sarge holding a Taser. Joel Morris.

She had no gun, no weapon of any kind, but she didn't care. Joel had hurt, maybe killed, the two beings she cared about more than anything else in the world.

"Stop right there."

Joel lifted his head. Green eyes caught and held the light. She moved toward him but hesitated when he bolted to his feet. Facing her as he backed up, he aimed the stun gun at her. Where had he gotten that? Both Sarge and David were shaking and immobilized from the jolt of electricity they'd received.

She held her hands up and backed far enough away that the stun gun wouldn't reach her.

"You will pay for thinking you could catch me, detective." He stepped toward her. His hand on the finger of the stun gun.

There was noise up the hallway—the sound of people, maybe coming this way.

Joel lifted his chin at the noise, turned and

ran in the opposite direction, disappearing around a corner.

Maya chased after him. She entered a long hallway but Joel was nowhere in sight. She ran back to where Sarge and David lay. There were no people in the hallway. They must have turned down a different way. At least the potential of a crowd had scared Joel away before he could hit her with the stun gun.

David had stopped shaking but had not yet sat up. Sarge's legs still spasmed.

Maya grabbed David's radio off his belt and notified Noah where Joel was headed. She jumped up and ran down the hallway where she had just come from, calling for the nurse, and then returned to be with David and Sarge.

David was sitting up but looked very pale. Her K-9 partner had stopped quivering but still lay on his side, making yipping sounds that indicated he was in pain.

She handed David's radio back to him.

David's hands were shaking when he took the radio. "Thank you."

Maya drew her attention to her partner. She made soothing sounds. She petted his head and then along his back and stomach. Despite the pain and shock he must be going through, Sarge's tail thumped on the carpet when she touched him.

"Poor guy," David said. "It takes a while for the effects of the stun gun to wear off. I still feel like I am vibrating from the inside."

She rested Sarge's head in her lap. "And it doesn't make any sense to him." Part of police training at the academy involved being zapped with the stun gun, so Maya knew what it felt like.

The nurse came around the corner. "What happened?"

"These two were hit with a stun gun."

Her eyes widened. "Well, let's get you to an exam room." She looked at David. "Do you feel well enough to walk?"

"I'll be fine. It just takes a bit to feel normal. I don't need a doctor to look at me."

"What about the dog?" The nurse's voice filled with compassion as she stepped closer.

Maya stroked Sarge's head. She hated seeing him like this. "Let's just give him a minute. The stun gun doesn't do any permanent physical damage. I guess I yelled for you because I was so afraid when I saw these two just lying on the carpet, so disabled."

"Okay, then," the nurse murmured. "Let me know if you need anything." She headed back down the hall.

"I heard you talking to Noah," David said,

reattaching his radio to his belt. "Maybe he'll spot Joel."

"The only reason that creep is coming out of hiding is to come after me and you. So far Hans has not spotted him on any of the security cameras."

"He knows the ship pretty well and he must be finding ways to avoid the cameras."

She nodded. "He must have a hiding place. Any ideas?"

"After I saw your text, I thought about that." David shook his head. "He would have access to all the areas that are for the crew members only. But there could be an empty cabin he managed to get into."

Sarge lifted his head and whimpered. Joy surged through Maya. "Hey buddy, welcome back." She rubbed his ears.

David reached out to pet him. "He growled right before the attack. Things could have been a lot worse if he hadn't been with me."

Sarge got to his feet and licked Maya's cheek. "I always feel like he has my back. I couldn't ask for a better partner. How did Joel get a stun gun anyway?"

"Hans texted me a while back that he'd taken off his belt to jump into a pool to help when a developmentally disabled who had been drowning started to pull the lifeguard under with him. When he put the belt back on the stun gun was gone."

"That makes our perp that much more dangerous."

Both David and Maya petted the now fully revived Sarge. Their hands touched. Maya gazed into David's eyes as she felt a spark of awareness between them. Maybe it was just because she'd seen both her dog and the man she had to admit she cared about deeply in such a vulnerable state. All the same, she could not deny she had feelings for this man.

David slowly stood up "Come on, the three of us have a job to do." He held a hand out to help Maya to her feet.

When he grasped her hand, warmth spread up her arm and was like a zap of electricity to her heart. She glanced at him and quickly looked away, feeling her cheeks grow hot. Why did he make her feel like some sort of shy junior high girl?

David had turned to head up the hallway. She reached out for his arm, touching his elbow. "I'm just glad you and Sarge are okay. That was pretty scary to see you both lying on the floor like that." Her voice sounded breathless, but she didn't care.

David studied her for a moment. The blue sparkle in his eyes grew a little duller. "All in the line of duty, right?" His voice had no emotion at all.

Just like that he threw cold water on her feelings. "Yeah…right…sure." Her tone of voice did not hide her disappointment.

SIXTEEN

As he turned to head up the hallway, David cringed at his icy response to Maya. She had merely expressed that she cared about him... and that scared him. What would it mean to open his heart to a woman? It meant he could be hurt again. Not a chance he wanted to take.

Until she'd come into his life, he had liked his floating world with the ever-changing scenery. He'd felt a sense of purpose in knowing it was his job to keep the people on board safe. Now everything had gone sideways because if he was honest with himself, he cared about her too.

The realization made David walk even faster as if he could outrun his feelings.

"Slow down... Sarge and I can't keep up with you."

"Sorry, I'm just thinking that time is running short for catching Joel." That wasn't entirely true. Even though he was frustrated by the guy's ability to evade them, the fast walking had nothing to do with the manhunt they were in the midst of.

Maya and Sarge came alongside him. "So how do we find out if there are any empty cabins in the crew area?"

"We can check with the lady who makes those assignments. She's one deck up in a little administrative office."

As they walked side by side toward the elevator, he kept stealing glances in Maya's direction. Despite all his resistance, she had somehow managed to tap into some part of his heart that he'd thought had gone dormant. The part that wanted to love and give.

They rode the elevator up and David led them to the information office. The woman behind the desk smiled when she saw him. Juanita Dickens May was a woman in her sixties who had worked for the Alaska Dream cruise line in some capacity since she was twenty. David always felt like they understood each other in wanting to call the ship home and she had become a substitute mom for him in many ways.

"David, always good to see you! I have cookies I made myself in the crew kitchen if you're interested." Juanita stood up. "They are just in the back room."

"I wish I had time. We're kind of in the middle of something that can't wait."

"I've been watching those bulletins up on the newsfeed. I hope you catch the predator who has made it unsafe for women to be alone on the ship." Juanita drew her attention to Maya and Sarge. "Looks like you have some help with your search. Would your dog like a treat?"

David smiled at the offer. Juanita had treats for everyone of every age and species.

"It's better that the dog not have anything right now," Maya said. Sarge sat down beside her and looked up at Juanita.

The older woman studied Maya and then glanced in David's direction. Juanita was not dumb. She'd probably figured out that Maya wasn't just a passenger with a service dog. "You've done a good job, David, at not triggering panic but keeping passengers safe."

The compliment warmed him all the way to the marrow. "Thank you, Juanita. Which brings me to the reason we're here. We need to check on cabin vacancies in the crew quarters."

"I don't have to look. I can tell you right now that there are no vacancies in the crew quarters. Some have only one person when there is room for two. We were full up when we left Seattle. We had only one person quit last minute."

That one employee must be the woman who broke up with Joel. "Can I get her name and contact information?"

"Sure." Juanita bustled to her keyboard.

"Maybe it would be worth it to make a ship to shore call to the ex-girlfriend. She might be able to shed light on where Joel would be hiding."

The older woman handed David a printout. "When you're less busy, we'll have to grab a bite. See you at church on Sunday."

David took the printout. "Thanks, Juanita. For sure, we'll get a coffee or something soon."

As they left the office, Maya piped up. "They have a church on the ship?"

"It's kind of informal. There are about thirty of us who meet in the all-purpose conference room. We have a guitar player and Juanita has a beautiful singing voice."

"That's neat. You do have fellowship. Here I thought you were some sort of lone ranger Christian."

David laughed. "There's a lot you don't know about me."

"And Juanita is kind of like your shipboard mom." Maya's voice got quieter. "You have a nice life here."

Had Maya come to a place of acceptance that there couldn't be anything between them? Somehow that made him really sad. The turmoil he felt caused his stomach to twist into a knot. "Maybe when all this is over, and Joel is behind bars, you can take a cruise and actually enjoy yourself."

"That sounds fun. I'd like that. If I can engineer some time off work and save the money."

"I think as a thank-you I might be able to talk the owner into comping you."

Maya stopped walking and faced David. "I'm not sure why you're inviting me?"

He was quick with his answer, realizing how misleading the offer had sounded. "As a friend and as a thank-you for all your help." At the same time, there was a part of him that wanted a chance to see her again once the case was wrapped up and things calmed down. He clenched his jaw. It felt like his emotions were swinging one way and then the other, making it seem like he was teasing Maya, which hadn't been his intent at all.

Before she could respond, David's radio buzzed. He pushed the talk button. "Go ahead, Noah."

"I've searched all the possibilities in crew headquarters, laundry, storage, even the dining hall and kitchen. There was some evidence in one of the linen storage closets that someone may have slept in there, but no one, including the roommate, has seen any sign of him. However, all the other crew members know to be on the lookout for Joel."

"I doubt he'll come back to that linen closet now." David took a deep breath to stave off the mounting frustration. "Look you must be tired. Why don't you get some shut-eye?"

"I just need an hour or so and then I'll come back on duty."

"Let me know when you are rested and ready. Over and out." David put his radio back on his belt. He stared at the piece of paper Juanita had given him and read the name Tiffany Swarthout. He'd seen the name before when they'd been looking to see if any employees had quit. "Let's make this phone call. Right now, it's our only lead for finding Joel before it's too late."

As David, Maya and Sarge returned to the security office to make the call to Joel's ex-girlfriend, Maya found herself wrestling with confusion about David. He'd invited her back to the ship when things would be more relaxed while making it clear that the invitation was purely platonic in nature. Given her feelings, she wasn't sure if she could just be his friend.

It led only to heartache to hold out hope that
when a man said he wanted to be friends that
perhaps it could turn into something more.

When they entered the security office, Hans
was still watching the screens.

"You look wiped. Why don't you take a
break?"

"Good idea." Hans rubbed the back of his
neck and turned his head side to side. "So do
you have any new leads?"

David held up his phone. "I'm hoping this
phone call might help us narrow down our
search. It's Joel's ex-girlfriend. We think she
might be the reason he went off the deep end
and started attacking women."

Hans nodded. "Let me know what you two
come up with." He retreated to the back room
and closed the door.

David sat down and placed the phone on the
counter. "I'll put her on speaker so you can
hear the conversation."

Maya took a chair, determined to stop thinking about David in a romantic way and focus
on catching Joel. She hadn't come on board the
ship to fall for someone—she'd been hired to
do a job and she needed to get it done.

David punched in the number. He set the
phone down on the counter by the security
screens.

She did a quick study of the security screens, still hoping that Joel would make an appearance.

After three rings, a voice came on the line. "Hello?"

David leaned toward the phone. "Is this Tiffany Swarthout?"

"Yes, what's this about?"

"This is David Garrison, chief of security on the Alaska Dream cruise ship out of Seattle. I understand you used to be an employee here."

"That's right," Tiffany answered.

"May I ask why you quit?"

There was a long pause but then she said, "I quit to get away from my then boyfriend."

"Joel Morris?"

"Yes. Why do you ask? Has something happened?"

"We have reason to believe that Joel is responsible for some attacks on women on the ship…and a murder."

A gasp came across the line. "I'm so sorry to hear that! I knew I had to get away from him. He scared me. But I—I had no idea he would go after other women."

"Why did he scare you?"

"Joel was wonderful at first. The attention, the flattery and the gifts made me feel so special. But then if I even talked to another guy, even on the job, he would get mad. I started to see a side of him that made me afraid. He was possessive and controlling." A tense silence filled the air. When she spoke again Tiffany's voice was raw with pain. "But when he got physical, I knew I needed to get away fast."

That made sense to Maya. Joel had probably always been unstable, but it came out only in intimate relationships like a romance. "Hi Tiffany, this is Maya Rodriguez. I'm helping with the investigation. Had Joel said anything about past relationships?"

"He had nothing but negative things to say about other women, including his mother. That should have been a red flag," Tiffany said. "Please, if I had known he was going to hurt other women… I don't know, maybe I should have done something."

"Tiffany, don't beat yourself up," Maya said. "Right now, we want to focus on getting Joel into custody."

"Thank you for saying that. I want to help any way I can. It's important that Joel not hurt anyone ever again. What can I do?"

"Joel's hiding somewhere on the ship. We think that you might be able to help us find him. Was there any special place he may have taken you that he might be using as a hideout?"

Tiffany didn't answer right away. "We used

to meet on the upper deck at night after our shifts. Hardly anyone goes up there. It was private."

Maya thought it would be better not to tell her about the attacks and murder on the upper deck. She seemed eaten up with guilt as it was. "Anything else you can remember would be helpful, Tiffany. Even if it doesn't seem important."

"I'm just trying to think of something that might be helpful," Tiffany said. "He had worked on that ship for a long time… He knew lots of clandestine places." The silence indicated that she was searching her memory. "Oh wait. I do remember something. You know that entertainment venue, the really big one where they have the musical reviews and concerts?"

"On deck seven?" David's voice held a note of hope.

"Yes, the one with a catwalk. Anyway, Joel took me up there late at night after the venue was shut down. He knew the code to get in there through the back way where the performers enter."

"Tiffany, that may help us," he said. "If you remember anything else, please get in touch with us right away."

"I will. I had no idea Joel was capable of killing someone." Tiffany's voice faltered.

It sounded like she was feeling a lot of anguish. "Tiffany, we don't blame you in any way. You did the right thing in protecting yourself."

They said their goodbyes and David clicked the phone off. "Go wake up Hans. We might need his help."

Maya hurried into the break room and shook Hans's shoulder. "So sorry to disturb you. We might have a lead on where Joel is hiding out."

Hans sat up, blinking rapidly. "Give me just a second."

When she returned to the main room of the security office, David was clicking away on the computer keyboard. He stared at the screen. "The last show for that theater shut down over two hours ago. They do family-friendly stuff, so they are not going all night." He grabbed his phone and pressed in a number. "I have a master key to get in. I just need to get the permission of the guy who manages that theater."

While David made the call, Hans stumbled out of the break room. Still looking a little sleepy.

"Long night for all of us, huh?" he said, glancing toward David who had just hung up the phone. "So what's the plan?"

David motioned for Maya and Hans to move

in closer as he pointed at the computer screen. "I've got a rough map of the theater that is in all the guides for the ship. It's a big theater with two entrances for the public and two for the entertainment at the back."

Maya stared at the screen. In addition to the rows of seats, there was a balcony. "There must be dressing rooms, right?"

"Yes. They are not shown but they are off to either side of the stage. Plus, there's a costume and prop storage room here next to the women's dressing room."

Hans leaned closer to the screen. "Lot of places someone could hide."

"Hans I want you to enter through one of the public entrances. Maya and I along with Sarge will each come through the back way."

"Got it," Maya and Hans spoke in unison.

As they got prepared to leave and head toward the theater, that familiar mixture of anticipation and fear coursed through Maya. When she worked with the rest of the K-9 team, the intensity of emotion was the same.

As they hurried down corridors toward the theater, she wished they had guns. Even though there were three of them and only one suspect, she was keenly aware of how vulnerable she felt going into a potentially volatile situation unarmed.

SEVENTEEN

As they got closer to the theater, they slowed down from a jog to a brisk walk. Though his injured leg was hurting, David relished the excitement of moving in on a suspect. He swiped the card that would open the door for Hans. He cupped the other man's shoulder. "Go in on my command. It's best that we all enter at the same time. Give Maya and me a few minutes to get around to the back. I'll radio you when we're in place. The doors have been reprogrammed so you can't get out without a card key. If he's in there, we can trap him."

Hans nodded while he held on to the door David had just swiped. He had it open less than an inch. Not enough so anyone would notice it was open. Hans gave David a quick salute. "Got it."

David's heart was already pounding from the run to the theater and the anticipation of catching Joel. He led Maya to the door she was to enter and unlocked it for her. "You don't have a radio, but I'll step back from the door and give you a hand signal that I'm going in."

She nodded and gazed at him with such trust in her eyes. While Sarge stood at attention looking up at him. Maybe it was just the adrenaline coursing through his system, but he felt so drawn to her in the moment that he reached up and grazed her cheek with his fingers. "Stay safe."

He sprinted to the other door and unlocked it. With the door only ajar a sliver, he peered inside not seeing or hearing anything. He looked around for something to brace the door in place so he could signal Maya without losing time unlocking the door again. Just inside the door was an empty shoe box. He grabbed the top of the box to hold the door in place and then he radioed Hans. "We're in place, give me a five count before you go in. Go slow. If he is in there, we don't want to alarm him. Our best chance of catching him is if we can surprise him. Maybe we'll get lucky and he'll be sleeping. Let's keep radio silence for now unless you see him."

"Got it," Hans said.

David took several steps back and craned his neck. Maya was staring in his direction waiting for his signal. She must have braced her door as well.

He lifted and dropped his hand making as big a motion as possible so she could see him in the dim light. She disappeared. David bolted toward the door and eased his way inside where it was even darker. He had come in on the side of the men's dressing room. As his eyes adjusted to the dim light, he saw the sign on the door. The dressing room was unlocked. He eased the door open and peered inside. It was an open room with makeup tables and mirrors. Not many places to hide.

David stepped outside into the hall that led to the backstage area. When he peered out onto the stage whose front curtain was open, he could just make out Hans as he searched the theater seats and then headed up to the balcony. David's gaze was drawn upward to the catwalk and the rows of lights. He didn't see movement anywhere.

Still remaining hidden behind the back curtain, he peered across the empty stage expecting to see Maya. He waited a few seconds more before becoming worried. She should have cleared both the dressing and costume rooms by now.

Aware that Joel could be anywhere in the theater, David slipped behind the back curtain to avoid being seen. Concerned, he hurried across the stage to check on Maya.

Maya cleared the women's dressing room fairly quickly, but the costume room proved to be more of a chore. There were a hundred nooks, crannies and closets where someone could hide. Sarge sniffed around, alerting to something in the corner behind a rack of costumes.

Even with Sarge to help her, she was keenly aware of how vulnerable she was without a weapon. Even though Joel had dropped the hunting knife, he worked in a kitchen and could have stolen one of the chef's knives easily enough.

She called toward where Sarge had alerted. "Ship security. Stay where you are."

Sarge sat back on his haunches and let out a single sharp bark. She relaxed a little. If there had been a person back there, he would have remained standing and kept barking. She hurried to where Sarge had alerted.

When she peered behind the rack of costumes, she found what looked like a makeshift bed fastened from some costumes and a blanket and a take-out food container. Evidence that Joel had probably been there recently. He'd have to be out by early afternoon the next day when the actors and tech people showed up to get ready for the evening shows. She was starting to get a picture of how Joel must be evading them by moving from place to place at different times of the day when he knew certain parts of the ship would be closed down. Her guess was that if he hadn't hidden the evidence of his staying here, he hadn't left. That meant that he was still somewhere in the theater. She tensed at the thought.

The door burst open.

She whirled around. Even though he was dressed in black just like she was, his stature gave David away.

"I was worried when you didn't show backstage."

"He's been here, and I think he's still in the theater." She pointed to the makeshift bed.

David stepped in to look. "Let me alert Hans." He pulled his radio off his belt, then spoke in a whisper. "Hans, are you there? We think the suspect is on the premises." David took his finger off the talk button. He glanced nervously at Maya. Sarge let out a yip. He spoke into the radio again. "Hans, are you there?"

A tension-filled silence fell between them.

"Do you think Joel got to him?"

David shook his head. "Not sure. But if Joel

did get to Hans, it means he know we're in here looking for him."

"Maybe he silenced his radio because he saw Joel, and he didn't want the noise to mess with his chances of catching him."

"Maybe," David said. "We're dealing with a bunch of unknowns. All the same, move slowly and try not to be detected. I'm sure Sarge will sound the alarm if you find Joel. I'll get to you as fast as I can."

She nodded. "I'll take stage left and work my way up to the balcony. You can take stage right. We'll meet in the balcony."

David nodded. "Let's do this." He disappeared from sight. She could hear his feet padding softly as he hurried to the other side of the theater.

Maya searched the backstage area and then took the steps down to the auditorium where she pressed against a wall. Sarge remained close beside her as they inched along. She gazed down the rows of seats, knowing that Joel could be hiding in any one of them. A chill raced down her spine as flashes of his previous attacks assailed her, but nothing would deter her. She had a job to do.

Working her way to the end of the auditorium, she pushed open the swinging doors that led to the lobby. Maya could see David on the other side of the lobby though he was mostly a moving shadow. She saw him only because she was looking for him. Other than the ticket booth, there was no place in the lobby to hide. Heart pounding, she sprinted the short distance to the ticket booth. She peered through the window half expecting Joel to jump up at her. When she tried the door to the ticket booth it was locked. That settled that.

David came toward her. "We've got to find Hans. He's still not responding by radio. The last place I saw him was the balcony. Let's head up there."

They separated and Maya hurried back into the auditorium with Sarge. She found the winding staircase to the balcony and headed up. She stepped out onto the balcony and searched the seats while she moved toward the back. Opposite her, David had made his way to the very back of the balcony and was moving down row by row.

A light on the stage burst on. Maya turned around. Sarge growled. Someone lay face down on the stage with a spotlight on him. Maya froze in place. It was Hans and he wasn't moving.

Quelling a rising panic, David hurried down the balcony stairs and raced toward the stage where his colleague lay, maybe unconscious, maybe dead. It was clear now Joel was in the theater and he was playing a sick game with them.

He bolted toward the stage fully aware that Joel might be watching them.

David's primary concern was for Hans, but he also thought maybe the perp might be setting some kind of trap. His attention was drawn upward to the rows of stage lights that must weigh a ton. He got to the base of the stage, standing at the bottom of the stairs that led up. His gaze moved across the auditorium where Maya and Sarge were. They'd slowed down as well. Hans still had not moved. David's chest grew tight at the sight of his prone partner. And then he saw the pool of blood around Hans's head. Forgetting the risk, David bolted up the stage reaching out for the injured officer.

A force came at him from behind, knocking him off his feet while a bolt of electricity shot through him. David was momentarily paralyzed. He could hear Sarge barking and feel the sensation that Joel was reaching into his chest pocket.

As he lay unable to move, he heard retreating footsteps headed toward one of the backstage doors. Maya was right beside him. She shouted at him as she ran past him. "He took your card key. That was all he wanted."

David was still extremely disoriented. Joel had known he was trapped and outnumbered. Escape was the only option and now he had a master card key. Knowing that Maya and Sarge were in hot pursuit of Joel, David drew his attention to Hans as he waited for the effect of the stun gun to wear off.

With the spotlight on, he could see that the other man was still breathing. He reached out and touched the puddle of blood by Hans's head. He drew it up to his nose expecting that coppery smell. It wasn't blood at all, red dye or something like it from the prop room.

He reached out to Hans, lifting his closed eyelids. Something had caused him to lose consciousness even if he wasn't bleeding. Hans's radio was not on his belt. Joel must have taken it. David grabbed his own radio and called for a medic. "I've got an officer who needs medical attention. Deck seven. The stage of the main entertainment venue."

"We're on our way. Be there in five."

"Thanks."

He rose to his feet and stepped toward the door where Maya and Sarge had gone chasing after Joel. The hallway was dark, though he could see lights at the end of it where it connected with the public part of the ship. He ran to the end of the hallway and peered out, not seeing Maya or Joel. There were still a few people strolling around. Some of the shops stayed open late as did the bars and buffets.

He needed to get back and make sure Hans was taken care of. Once he was back on the stage where the officer still lay motionless, it took only a few more minutes before the EMTs arrived.

David leaned over while the medic was checking Hans out and taking his vitals. "Don't be alarmed. The blood is not real."

The EMT gave Hans a quick-once over. Then rolled Hans on his back and lifted his eyelids. "He might have sustained a blow to the head." The EMT turned back toward his partner. "Let's get him on the stretcher."

David watched them transport Hans. He'd have to check in with the doctor in a bit. Knowing that Joel would be privy to all radio communication, David called Noah on the phone and told him he needed to get back on shift. "Meet me in the security office and we'll come up with a strategy. He's got a master card key. That means he has access to a ton more places." Fortunately, it was a different master card key that gave David access to passenger rooms and could be used only if the safety of the passenger was at risk. The key that Joel had taken would get him into any shop or public area that was locked after hours. It also gave him access to supply closets where merchandise was stored.

He had just moved to step off the stage and head out the backstage entrance when Maya came through the door with Sarge right beside her. She spoke between breaths, shaking her head. "We lost him."

"Where at?"

"He went down a corridor where there are a bunch of niche shops that are not open late. He probably went into one of the shops and the door locked behind him. If Joel was still carrying that knife, Sarge could have sniffed him out."

David knew the area that Maya was talking about. Joel could have taken a side hallway as well. "Let's get up to the security office— maybe we can see him on camera. I'm going to send Noah out so we can catch our breath and grab a quick bite. This could take all night."

"How is Hans?"

"Not sure. I'll check in with the doctor later," David said. "Joel took Hans's radio. So all communication will be via phone. We don't want Joel knowing what our next step is."

They hurried back to the security office.

David had communicated with Noah where to begin his search. David put on a pot of coffee and grabbed some granola bars from a cupboard above the microwave. Maya was already sitting in front of the security monitors clicking through them and shaking her head.

He placed the granola bar on the counter in front of her. "Thanks." Her fingers tapped the keyboard as she switched from one camera to another to see what was going on.

"Why are you shaking your head?"

"It feels like we're doing the same thing over and over and Joel keeps getting the upper hand." She lifted her hands from the keyboard and leaned closer to the monitors. "Some of these screens are black." She put her fingers back on the keyboard and clicked around to bring up the different screens.

David drew his attention to the black screens. "He's disabling the cameras." He clenched his jaw. "At least we know where he's been. By the time we could get Noah there, Joel will have moved on."

"We're running out of time, David. What we're doing is not working." She looked back at the screens. "And now it's like he's toying with us."

"What are you suggesting?"

Maya swiveled in her chair. "I think we need to set a trap, and I think I need to be the bait."

EIGHTEEN

Even as Maya proposed the plan to catch Joel, she had to fend off the rising fear. Sarge looked up at her and made a whimpering noise.

David didn't answer right away. He straightened up and looked at the black screens. "I don't like the idea of putting you at risk."

"How many more hours do we have until we are in port?"

"We'll get in early morning in about six hours." David shook his head. "I don't know if it will even work to set a trap. All he has to do is hide out until we dock."

"So our last chance to get him would be before he leaves the ship?"

"Right. We can make sure security is high when we dock, but I'm concerned he'll be able to give us the slip, considering how much skill he has displayed so far."

"We know that he has a thing for that upper deck. It's been closed off and there are no cameras up there. What has it been… More than a day since he tried to attack a woman other than me? I say that his anger is mostly directed at me because I am trying to keep him from hurting other women. What I know about my training in criminal psychology tells me he will need to try to get to me again soon. It's like a compulsion."

David ran his hands through his hair.

She could tell he still wasn't convinced. "Look, David. I don't want to do this either. But I want to catch this guy. Which means I have to look totally vulnerable. So Sarge can't be there."

"I don't like it, Maya. You'll be risking your life."

The plan was becoming clearer in her mind. "He's smart enough to know to look for you and the rest of the security team. You can't be anywhere close. Is there a way we could set up hidden cameras so you guys see what was going on if I did need help?"

"How would we get to you fast enough? Besides, we don't have extra security cameras."

"All of that would have to be worked out." Maya felt an increasing tension in her muscles as she thought about what she was proposing. "I just don't know if there are any other options at this point."

David's phone buzzed. He took it out of his pocket. As Maya listened to one side of the conversation, it was clear that Noah had spotted either Joel or some evidence of the killer's whereabouts. David ended the conversation by saying. "Okay, we'll get there as fast as we can."

He clicked off his phone. "A passenger called in that they thought they saw someone in the bumper car area which is shut down right now. If it's Joel, it's going to take all three of us to catch him. Let's go. I need to think about your plan some more, Maya. There has to be another way."

She shoved Sarge's leash toward David. "You take him. That way while we're searching, I'll look super vulnerable. Joel cannot control his impulse to go after women who remind him of Tiffany. Maybe he'll come after me while we are looking for him."

"Maya, we've got to do this in an organized way. Security measures need to be in place to ensure you'll be safe."

"We're running out of time. And I do have self-defense training. All we need to do is lure him out." Given Joel's previous attacks, David's concerns were not unfounded. But the thing foremost in her thoughts was catching Joel. Maya hurried toward the elevator that would take them to the deck where the bumper cars were. She held the door for Sarge and David.

She was afraid the few minutes in the elevator would give David time to make more objections about the danger she was putting herself in. However, before he could speak, his phone rang again. It was clear it was Noah once more. David gave single word responses and then ended with. "Okay, we'll widen the search."

Clicking off his phone, he turned toward Maya. "Noah says he found disabled cameras in the bumper car area. We're going to widen the search to the areas around the bumper cars. He is searching the north end. We'll take south and east."

"We are running out of time David. We need to split up. I'll be okay."

David didn't answer right away. Finally, he nodded. "You move toward the arcade. Widen your search as you clear each area." David handed her the leash. "You're vulnerable enough as it is. Take your partner with you."

As she held Sarge's leash, Maya wrestled with a mixture of relief and frustration. If Joel saw that Sarge was with her, he would be less likely to come at her knowing that he'd been foiled by the dog before. But having her partner close made her feel that much safer. The elevator doors slid open.

"Remember, I'm a phone call away," David said as they stepped out.

"I know." Her throat went tight. The time it took to make the call was enough time for Joel to kill her. If she could even get to the phone fast enough.

David reached out and touched her arm. "I'm afraid for you."

She tilted her head to look into his eyes. The concern she saw in his expression compelled her to fall into his arms. "I'm scared too."

He held her for a long moment. Drawing strength from his embrace, she closed her eyes and relished how safe it felt to be in his arms. She pulled back.

He leaned and kissed her on the forehead. "We're in this together. I have your back."

Still reeling from the intensity of his hug and the light touch of his lips on her skin, she nodded. "You have to give me some credit. I do have police training."

They ran toward the bumper cars and then split off. Maya saw the sign for the arcade which was next to the bumper cars. She could see the bumper cars through the glass walls.

Movement and shadow on the other side must be Noah searching the area.

She stepped toward the arcade but was surprised to find the door unlocked. Maya clicked David's number. She spoke in a whisper. "I'm outside the arcade. It's not locked."

"I'm coming your way."

She looked up to where a security camera was still in place. Maybe someone had just forgotten to lock the arcade. Most of the security cameras were up high enough that Joel must have some sort of long object to reach up and disable them. His motive was probably to make their search for him that much harder, but it also left a trail of where he'd been. It was like he was playing a game of cat and mouse with the security team.

She glanced through the windows of the arcade again. Lights flashed on one of the games that had a moment ago been dark. Her heart pounded as adrenaline surged through her body. Joel was in there or had been only seconds ago. If she was going to catch him, she couldn't wait for backup. Maya stepped inside with Sarge beside her. She searched for an exit door.

The arcade was long and narrow. She spotted the exit sign nearly hidden behind a tall game but could still see the flashing lights of the game in her peripheral vision. After running toward the exit, she pushed open the door, then found herself staring down the short hallway where she could see a sliver of the bumper car area. An odd banging sound caught her attention.

She took in a deep breath. Sarge stood at attention watching her and waiting for a command. Her partner's response gave her courage and quieted her fear. She moved toward the bumper car area. Through the glass, she could see that someone had started two of the bumper cars, so they were banging into each other over and over. Lights flashed on the cars each time they collided. Clearly, this was Joel's work. There was something menacing about the repetitive noise.

"Maya?"

David's voice reverberated behind her and she whirled around.

"I thought I could catch him." She had a feeling Joel was long gone by now.

David held a small piece of paper. "This was on the flashing game in the arcade." He handed her the piece of paper.

The message was in block letters with a red pen.

I will get you, Maya.

* * *

Even in the dim light, David could see all the color drain from Maya's face as she held the threatening note.

She kept her eyes on the note. "You know what I'm feeling right now?"

"Fear would be understandable," David said.

She looked up and shook her head. "What I feel now is righteous anger. Joel thinks he has the upper hand. And now he thinks he can torment me. He's a criminal and he needs to be behind bars."

Through the glass windows to the bumper cars, David could see Noah shutting off the two cars that were banging into each other. The other man shook his head, indicating that he had not found any sign of Joel.

"David, we *have* to set a trap for Joel with me as the bait. It's the only way."

He signaled for Noah to come join them. David knew what Maya was saying was true. He just didn't want to think about the risk she would be taking. "We have to find a way to make sure you will be safe."

"Don't you see? Joel isn't stupid. If you are close by, he'll figure it out. I have to look totally exposed." She held up the piece of paper. "This note indicates his obsession with me. We're dealing with a clever, unhinged man.

The only thing we have working for us is his desire to hurt, even kill me. I believe if he sees a chance, he will take it."

Noah came over and joined them. "This guy knows the ship really well. There are too many places for him to hide until we get into port. David, we've got to do something different."

Maya turned toward Noah. "We were just talking about that." She handed him the threatening note. "We think if Joel gets a chance, he will come after me."

"What Maya wants to do though is very dangerous," David muttered. "Joel will figure out if protection is close by."

"So we have to come up with a way to trick him," Maya said. "If I go up to the upper deck alone, I believe that he will follow me up there and look for a chance to attack me."

David addressed his comments to Noah. "The upper deck is where Joel and his girlfriend who dumped him used to go. It's a triggering location. Given that the murder and a number of attacks took place up there, we believe he has almost an uncontrollable impulse to go after any woman who looks like his former girlfriend when he is up there."

Noah rubbed his chin. "So, we have to have a way to keep eyes on Maya and get to her quickly without Joel figuring out the setup."

David started walking. "Let's head back to the security office."

They all started walking while they brainstormed a plan.

"If we position cameras on the upper deck, he'll figure it out," Maya warned.

"We have almost no additional surveillance equipment anyway. We'd have to work with whatever the electronics shop had." David shook his head in frustration. "He'd figure out he was being watched anyway. I feel like our hands are really tied here."

They continued toward an open area with a view of the water and mountains in the distance. The light in the distance was their port city of Seward. Maya stopped and Sarge sat down beside her. "David what about the North Star? You would have a view of the upper deck from there if it was up high enough right?"

"Probably," he replied. "But I couldn't get down fast enough to come to help you."

"We'd have to create some sort of relay system. Noah up in the North Star where he has a view of the deck. And then you hiding somewhere so you could get to me as quickly as possible...but not where Joel would ever figure out where you were."

"That might work," Noah said. "We take the North Star up with me in it. Put out a notice that says it's broken and locked in place, so Joel doesn't make the connection. And if I stay up there an hour or so before Maya goes out on the upper deck…"

"We know that Joel stalks his victims and waits for an opportunity. Before I head to the upper deck, I'll give him plenty of opportunity to see that neither Sarge nor David are close, but I will try to stay in public areas."

"If I see that Maya is in danger, I can text you, David." Noah's inflection indicated excitement about the plan.

Maya could tell from David's body language that he still wasn't on board with the plan. He crossed his arms and his jaw hardened. "I don't like the idea of Maya being so vulnerable. And can we even find a place where *A*, Joel won't figure out I'm hiding and *B*, I can get to Maya fast enough."

They were standing outside the security office. David swiped his card key.

"Are there blueprints or a map of the ship that would show details, possible hiding places?" While she understood David's resistance and even was touched by how protective he was of her, she felt like they were running out of options and his stubbornness was costing them valuable time.

"The maps are very general, drawn up for

the passengers. I would need to go up to the upper deck and scout it out."

David seemed to be coming around.

"You two figure out the details," Noah said. "I need to get into position. I've got to track down the operator for the North Star. Text me the exact plan. If I need to be up there for a while, we don't have a lot of time."

Noah took off.

They stepped into the security office. David shook his head. "I'm not totally on board with this plan."

She gazed at him. "It's the only way."

"I got a text from Hans that he is out of the infirmary. I'm going to have him watching the security cameras that are still operational. After what he's been through, I think he needs to be at a desk. He can contact us if he spots Joel. The safest thing for you would be to catch him before he even gets to the upper deck."

"I agree."

"After I check on Hans, Sarge and I are going to try to find a hiding place. Noah's only going to have a partial view of the upper deck, so you'll have to stay toward the east side."

"Got it," she said.

"I'm worried about you."

"Don't be. I can handle this."

He reached up and cupped her cheek. "I

know but I care about you...a lot." His features softened as light came into his eyes. He leaned in and kissed her, brushing his lips over hers.

When he pulled away, she was breathless. He left the office with Sarge in tow not saying another word. Maya collapsed into a chair, still lightheaded from the kiss. What did David mean by *I care about you a lot*? And then a kiss. How ambiguous. It wasn't *I love you*. It wasn't *I want to be with you*. She shook her head. Maybe David didn't even know what he was really feeling.

She was still thinking about the effect David's kiss had on her when Hans entered the security office ten minutes later.

"David called me. Guess my job is to watch the cameras," Hans said. "David hasn't texted you yet that he has a hiding place?"

She shook her head.

"Guess we wait then."

Maya took in a breath, trying to soften some of the tension in her muscles. "Yes, we wait. How are you doing?"

"I have a bit of a headache, but I'll be okay." Hans clicked through the screens turning on the ones that were not black. "We won't be able to replace the disabled cameras until we're in port."

She stared at the screens. One of them revealed that the North Star was already being fully elevated. She studied the other screens catching a glimpse of Sarge right before he was out of camera range as he trailed behind David on the leash. The location revealed that they were still about a five-minute walk from the upper deck.

She pointed to the screen where she'd seen David and Sarge. "There are no more cameras to show us where they have gone?"

"The only other one in that area has been disabled."

She pulled out her phone and set it on the counter. When she clicked on the screen, she saw she had a text from Helena Maddox, one of the other K-9 officers.

What a day I've had. Luna and I went looking for Eli's survivalist family that his godmother so desperately wants to locate. While looking in a remote area of Chugach State Park, I ran into two men and showed them photos of the Seaver family. They said they didn't know the Seavers, but I think they were lying. Later when I was leaving, I was shot at. I think we are getting close and that is making someone nervous.

Luna was Helena's Norwegian elkhound. Maya stared at the phone for a long moment and said a silent prayer that she would get back to shore alive to help track down the Seaver family before it was too late.

David walked the upper deck with Sarge, not finding any hiding place that wouldn't be obvious. His only option was a supply closet filled with lounge chairs. The closet was around the corner and down a hallway from where Maya would be standing. He'd have no visual on her at all. At a dead run, he estimated it would take him about a minute to get to Maya if she needed help. Sixty seconds was time enough to kill someone. Plus, there would be an additional time delay if Noah had to communicate what he was seeing.

The closet was stuffed so full he and Sarge had to squeeze in. His hands were pressed close to his side. It took some maneuvering to get the phone to his face after he dialed Maya's number.

She answered right away, "Yes."

The sound of her voice renewed the memory of the kiss they'd shared. Without intending to, his voice took on a smoldering quality. "Hey, I'm in place. When you get to the upper deck if you think that Joel is near, I need you to press in my number and keep it on so I can hear what is happening."

"I might not have time to do that if I wait until I hear him coming. What if I just turn it on when I get to the upper deck?"

Not having radios was proving to be a challenge. "Okay, Noah can give me the play-by-play via text up to that point. If Joel does show, I am worried that the delay for Noah to communicate what is happening will be too great. I can't see you from my hiding place."

"David, I know you're worried, but remember I am a trained police officer."

The warmth in her voice made his heart beat faster. He had not lied when he said he cared about her, but was there something even deeper between them?

"I know you can take care of yourself, Maya. I'm just making sure every precaution is in place."

"I'll leave the security office in about two minutes. I'll make my way toward the upper deck slowly. If Joel is watching, he'll have every chance to see me."

David gripped his phone a little tighter and breathed in a wordless prayer. "I'll let Noah know the plan is in place and that you are on your way."

"Got it." A silence fell between them, but Maya stayed on the line. "I care about you too, David." She hung up.

Her words seemed to reverberate in his head. Had she confessed her feelings just in case she was killed?

NINETEEN

After saying goodbye to Hans, Maya left the security office and headed toward the upper deck. She chose a path that would make her visible from a distance and where there were still cameras so Hans would be able to track her and alert the rest of the team if she was attacked. It was hard to say if Joel would even take the bait.

She walked past a room with wide open doors. Classical music spilled out and when she glanced inside, she saw a strobe light and ballroom dancers moving across the floor. Her eyes traveled up to the balconies that looked down on the promenade.

Though most of the shops had closed down, some restaurants and bars were still open. There were enough people to ensure that Joel wouldn't try anything unless he could remain hidden.

By the time she made her way to the upper deck, her heart was racing and sweat trickled past her temple. Before she got to the upper deck where the railing was, and where Noah would have eyes on her, she passed a family. A mom and dad and two girls who looked to be under the age of five. The father held one of the girls in his arms.

"Have fun. We'd thought we'd come up for the view of the stars since they opened the deck up, but it's a little too windy and cold," the father said.

Maya drew her coat around her. "Still a nice night though."

The older of the two girls held her mother's hand. She pointed at Maya with her free hand. "I saw you with your dog."

"Yes, that's Sarge. He's with a friend right now."

As the voices of the family and footsteps echoed and faded, she was keenly aware of how vulnerable she was without Sarge. She walked more slowly. When she glanced around, she didn't see the supply closet David and Sarge were hidden in. That made her nervous. It must not be very close. Her heart pounded a little faster.

She could see the railing up ahead not far from the spot where Crystal Lynwood had been killed and the other woman had been attacked. She walked past the lounge chairs, stopping for a moment to look at the entry door where Joel had probably escaped after the attacks. There were multiple ways to get to the upper deck. Maybe Joel wouldn't follow her.

She stepped toward the railing and gripped it. A gust of wind made her jacket balloon and then deflate. She looked over her shoulder and up. Though the twilight made it into a silhouette, she could see the elevated North Star where Noah was. Lights of the port city they were headed toward glowed in the distance.

Maya thought she heard a noise behind her by the lounge chairs where the other entrance to the upper deck was. She hurried back there but saw nothing in the dim light.

Returning to the railing, she peered out, listening to the sound of the waves. Her hand rested on the side pocket of her jacket where she'd put her phone. If Noah saw anyone moving toward her, he would alert David.

After waiting about five minutes, she began to wonder yet again if maybe Joel wasn't going to show. Would he just lie low until they were in port and then find a way to slip off the ship unnoticed? He had to know they would ramp up security as the passengers got off. But she had to believe that his compulsion to go after women who reminded him of the one who had rejected him would override common sense. It had so far. Attacking women on a ship where he could not hope to escape, only hide, held a high level of risk.

Maya stared up at the twinkling stars and the outlines of mountains in the distance. Why at such a moment did she wish David was standing beside her and that they were just sharing a tender moment together, not entrenched in a sting operation? Her feelings for him ran so deep. Would she go so far as to say she loved him? Maybe. The kiss had caught her off guard after all his resistance to anything romantic. She shook her head at the memory of how his lips felt on hers.

Her phone dinged. She pulled it out. The text was from Noah.

No sign of him from up here. You see anything?

She remembered the noise that had sounded like someone coming through the entryway by the lounge chairs. It could have been the wind jostling a lounge chair.

She texted back.

Not sure. Pretty quiet.

Maya stepped away from the railing. She'd never been good at doing nothing and that was what this operation had started to feel like. What if Joel had figured out they were setting him up and now he was stalking another woman on some other part of the ship? Yet as smart as he was, it didn't seem like he'd be able to decipher what they had in mind to catch him. If her classes on criminal psychology had taught her anything, the note he'd left in the arcade meant he was honed in on her.

Still, just standing around was hard to do.

After putting her phone in her pocket, Maya remembered the lounge where the other victim had been with the kind older couple. That was on the other side of the ship where the upper deck wrapped around. She glanced up at the North Star. Noah might not have a visual on her if she went over there.

She returned to the railing and stared out at the rolling sea. The wind had intensified. She thought she heard a banging sound somewhere close.

Maya ran to check the entrance by the lounge chairs and found the door was open and banging against the wall. The wind could have done that. All the same she approached with caution. Noah would be able to see her go toward the door, but she'd be hidden under the eaves once she reached to close the door.

Why take the chance?

Let the door bang in the wind.

A voice as cold as ice pelted her eardrums. "I'd told you I'd come for you."

She whirled around. Joel stood three feet from her grinning. He must have used the entrance by the lounge, or Noah would have seen him.

She reached into her jacket pocket, fumbling with her phone. Then she put her other hand in her pocket hoping Joel wouldn't figure out what she was doing. She couldn't find the button right button without looking. Noah would see Joel and signal David. That was her hope.

Joel lunged at her.

She angled away but her foot caught on a leg of the lounge chair and she fell forward. The stumble gave Joel the advantage. He grabbed her arm, yanking her back, and then pushed her toward the open door. Now they were both hidden by the eaves. Had Noah had time to register what was going on?

"It's over for you."

Joel pulled a knife out of his pocket forcing her to step backward through the open door or be stabbed. He must have taken it from the kitchen where he worked.

She turned to run down the stairs, but Joel grabbed the hem of her jacket. "Don't you dare run from me."

Still on the narrow landing, she turned, seeking to get the knife out of his hand before he could do any damage. She reached for it. They tussled. She managed to smash the back of his hand against the stairwell wall causing him to drop the knife. Metal banged on concrete as the knife slid down several stairs.

Joel's expression communicated rage. "You will die." He bared his teeth and slammed both hands against her chest and shoulder. She stumbled backward, unable to catch herself, and fell on her back.

Somewhere in the distance, she heard a dog barking. Sarge. The wind seemed to pick the bark up and carry it away. But they were coming for her.

Alarm spread across Joel's face. Turning, he grabbed the door and latched it. Probably some sort of emergency latch for when there was a storm.

The delay gave her time to get to her feet. She looked around for the knife but didn't see it. She hurried down the stairs. Above her, she heard banging noises that indicated David and Sarge were trying to open the door.

She had only run down four stairs when the banging stopped. David must have realized the futility of trying to break down the door.

As she ran, she could hear Joel's footsteps behind her.

She saw a door up ahead, though she couldn't remember where it led. She pushed it open and as a gust of wind hit her, she realized she was on a tiny exposed viewing deck. She glanced one way and then the other, spotting the door that would allow her to escape. Joel grabbed her from behind before she could get to the door.

He yanked her around, so she was facing him. He shoved his arm under her chin, pressing hard and backing her against the wall.

Maya wheezed, unable to breath due the pressure he put on her neck.

His eyes were wild and unfocused. "Having trouble breathing, my dear?"

She lifted her leg to kick him. The blow felt weak and only seemed to enrage him more. Now he grabbed her and banged the back of her head against the wall.

Pain radiated through her skull. Knowing that his favorite thing to do was choke her, she was ready for him when his hands reached for her neck. Maya deflected the move. "You won't get away with this."

"That's what all the pretty girls say." He grabbed her hair.

She heard barking.

The door opened a sliver. Joel kicked it then swung her body around so her back was against the door and his hand pinned her there by pressing into her shoulders. His face was so close to hers she could hear him breathing.

David was on the other side of the door trying to open it while the weight of her body held it in place. Sarge's barking intensified.

She scratched and clawed at Joel's hands while she leaned forward, hoping to allow David to get the door open.

Joel reached for her neck choking her, pressing harder and harder. She saw black dots and felt light-headed.

The door separated from the frame then banged shut again. Joel's grip on her neck loosened momentarily. She took in a breath and pushed off the door.

It opened again not more than a few inches.

Sarge's barking was the last thing she heard before the darkness surrounded her.

David managed to get the door open far enough for Sarge to squeeze through. The barking was filled with menace and punctuated with growls. David pushed hard against the door, but it was held in place.

On the other side of the door he heard Joel yelp in pain. David grabbed the knob and pushed on the door again. There was still some sort of weight on the other side, but he was able to open it wide enough so he could get through. Once in, he saw that the weight was Maya's unconscious body. The sight of her lying there so still was like a blow to his stomach that knocked the wind out of him.

He knelt down. She still had a pulse.

Both Joel and Sarge were nowhere in sight. He hurried toward the entrance that led up the stairwell toward the sound of the muffled barking. He swung the door open. Sarge had cornered Joel on the landing.

"Call him off." Joel's voice was filled with terror.

David hurried up the stairs. Sarge stopped barking but licked his chops and kept his eyes on his prey.

David pulled Joel's hands behind him and secured them with zip ties they used as cuffs. "You're going to be locked up for a long time for what you've done."

Joel jerked and lifted his chin. "We'll see about that."

Noah appeared at the bottom of the stairs.

"Take him in please," David said. "I've got to take care of Maya. Come on, Sarge."

David returned to where Maya still lay unconscious. Her head tilted to the side and her long dark hair covered her face.

He gathered her in his arms and brushed the hair away. Sarge whimpered and licked her face. "It's going to be all right. She's going to be okay. She has to be. I love her."

Sarge licked David's face and wagged his tail.

"It's true, buddy." He stared down at Maya's beautiful face. "I realized I loved her when I thought about a world without her if she didn't survive this operation to take down Joel..." He brushed his finger over her cheek.

Her eyes fluttered open. "David."

He gushed with joy. "So good to see you."

"Joel?"

"We caught him."

"Oh...good." Her voice was still very weak.

He cringed when he saw the bruises on her neck. "We almost lost you."

She looked directly at him. "Yes, but you didn't, and the important thing is that Joel has been apprehended."

"That is a great thing, but it's not the most important thing."

"What are you saying?"

David's throat constricted and his mouth went dry. He wanted to tell her he loved her but the words would not come. Sarge whimpered and licked David's hand as though offering support.

Maya lifted her head a little and then pushed herself into a sitting position. She glanced at the dog and then at David. "Is everything okay?"

"Great...fine."

"Well, once we're in port, Joel will be taken into custody and I can head back to headquarters in Anchorage. I missed everyone so much."

"I'm sure you're excited to get back." David rose to his feet and reached a hand down to help her to her feet.

"Sure of course."

They faced each other as the sun was coming up and the lights of Seward glowed in the distance. It was clear Maya had already shifted focus to getting back to work with her team. Even if he could find the words to tell her how he felt, she might not feel the same way.

TWENTY

The next day, before she could even make it to her office at headquarters with Sarge, Maya got a text from her boss.

Welcome back. We need you in the conference room ASAP.

Back to work. Though she was excited about seeing the rest of the team, she'd felt an emptiness ever since she'd said goodbye to David and left Seward. If he had truly cared about her, he would have said something, right?

Sarge trotted beside her as she headed to the conference room. "We just got to let him go, don't we? It wasn't meant to be."

Sarge whimpered in response.

When she entered the conference room, the first thing she saw was a banner that said Welcome Home, Maya.

Four team members stood around the conference table that held a box of cupcakes frosted in bright colors. Lorenza, her assistant Katie, Helena with her Norwegian elkhound Luna and Eli, the tech guy.

Helena stepped forward and gave Maya a hug. "The rest of the team is out on assignments. Otherwise everyone would have been here."

"It's good to be back," Maya said. Sarge let out a little yip. "He agrees."

Katie handed Maya a cupcake with yellow frosting.

Maya looked up at the sign.

I am home. And then she looked at the people surrounding the table. *And this is my family.*

Katie's green eyes flashed. "So you'll have to tell us all about your adventures on the cruise ship." She took a bite of her cupcake.

The sudden pang inside surprised Maya. She couldn't just forget David and get on with her life. Because the truth was, she cared deeply for him. If only he felt the same way… "Maybe sometime over lunch we will talk about it."

"I hate to rush this along," Lorenza said, running her hands through her silver hair. "But we do need to get to work. Maya, I want you and Helena to go back out to Chugach State Park where she was shot at after she started asking questions about Eli's godmother's family." Lorenza rested her gaze on Eli. "I think we are getting closer to finding the Seavers. Given what happened to Helena, I'm sending you out in pairs to ask questions."

Maya nodded, glad to be able to dive right into work. Maybe that would help ease her broken heart.

She and Helena loaded up into the K-9 trooper vehicle and headed out to the park. The day went by quickly. Though they questioned several people who were close to where Helena had been shot at, no new evidence emerged. They headed home just as the sun was setting. Maya was grateful for the longer days of summer.

Helena was driving as they pulled back into the headquarters parking lot. "You want to grab a bite?"

"Sure." Maya looked through the windshield. She wondered if her eyes were playing tricks on her. David, still dressed in his uniform, stood on the sidewalk holding a bouquet of flowers.

Helena leaned a little closer to the windshield. "Who's that handsome guy?"

Joy flooded through Maya. "Someone I met on the cruise." She clicked open her door and then unloaded Sarge. She raced over to where David waited.

He handed her the flowers. "I didn't go back out with the ship. I knew I couldn't."

She shook her head. "What are you saying?"

"Maya, when I thought you might die I realized something. I love you. I don't want to live in a world without you."

"But David, your life is on this ship."

"I can take a leave of absence and we can figure it out together. I'm open to anything as long as it's with you. Wherever you are is my home, Maya."

"I agree. You and me, together is all that matters." She looked down at her partner. "And Sarge of course."

He smiled. "Of course."

"Why the change of heart? You love that ship and your job. I saw that would never force you away from that."

"That's one of the reasons I love you Maya. Cause you want me to be happy." Light danced in his blue eyes. "After you left, I felt this huge hole inside." He brushed her cheek with the back of his fingers.

His touch made her feel warm all the way through. "Me too."

"I realized that what was holding me back had nothing to do with who you are. I can't let the fear that I will be like my father keep me from having love in my life. And I don't want to miss out on a lifetime with someone as wonderful as you."

Joy surged through her, and she reached up and wrapped her arms around his neck. "Oh David."

Being in David's arms made her feel alive.

He pulled his head back, smiled and kissed her.

His hand rested on her cheek as he looked into her eyes. "I love you and I want to be with you. That is all that matters."

"I love you too."

Sarge gave his bark of approval. David drew Maya close and kissed her again.

* * * * *

ALASKA K-9 UNIT
These state troopers fight for justice with the help of their brave canine partners.

Alaskan Rescue *by Terri Reed, April 2021*
Wilderness Defender
by Maggie K. Black, May 2021
Undercover Mission *by Sharon Dunn,*
June 2021
Tracking Stolen Secrets *by Laura Scott,*
July 2021
Deadly Cargo *by Jodie Bailey, August 2021*
Arctic Witness *by Heather Woodhaven,*
September 2021
Yukon Justice *by Dana Mentink,*
October 2021
Blizzard Showdown *by Shirlee McCoy,*
November 2021
Christmas K-9 Protectors *by Lenora Worth*
and Maggie K. Black, December 2021

Dear Reader,

Wow! What fun I had writing about danger and mystery on a cruise ship. I hope you enjoyed watching Maya, Sarge and David work together to track down a killer. As I was writing, I thought about how much fear has a hold on David's life. Because of past bad relationships and a father who was not a good role model, David is afraid of falling in love, of being hurt and of hurting someone else. In big ways and in small ways, fear can control our lives and we might not even realize it. We fear making a mistake or a bad decision, so we end up stuck doing nothing. I am one who is quick to beat myself up if things don't go well when I take action. I am learning to rewire my brain, so when something turns out different than I had intended, instead of condemning myself, I ask myself what can I learn from my mistake. That is where growth begins. How about you? Is fear holding you back in relationships, a job or in some other area of your life? Be courageous. God has not given us a spirit of fear.

Sharon Dunn

Get 4 FREE REWARDS!

We'll send you 2 FREE Books plus 2 FREE Mystery Gifts.

Harlequin Heartwarming Larger-Print books will connect you to uplifting stories where the bonds of friendship, family and community unite.

FREE Value Over $20

HARLEQUIN SELECTS COLLECTION

19 FREE BOOKS IN ALL!

From Robyn Carr to RaeAnne Thayne to Linda Lael Miller and Sherryl Woods we promise (actually, GUARANTEE!) each author in the Harlequin Selects collection has seen their name on the *New York Times* or *USA TODAY* bestseller lists!